"You and I have chemistry. And your plan to punish my father would yield a thousand percent more results if it was me you…"

He shot to his feet and moved toward her, and Jia's synapses gave out. That lizard part of her brain seemed to come awake, screaming *hot sexy man at twelve o'clock*. She craned her neck, just slightly, to look up into his face when he left only a foot or so between them.

"That's an interesting observation. Care to prove it?"

"Prove it…how?" she said, her throat suddenly dry. She should have known the beast would play with her.

"Kiss me. Then we will know if you're really a better proposition than—"

She pressed her hand to his mouth. Something hot and feral came awake in his gray eyes, something she hadn't even been sure he was capable of feeling.

"You should know, Jia," he said, wrapping long fingers around her wrist and tugging her hand away from his mouth. "Every game you begin, I will play, and play to win."

Tara Pammi can't remember a moment when she wasn't lost in a book—especially a romance, which was much more exciting than a mathematics textbook at school. Years later, Tara's wild imagination and love for the written word revealed what she really wanted to do. Now she pairs alpha males who think they know everything with strong women who knock that theory and them off their feet!

Books by Tara Pammi

Harlequin Presents

Returning for His Unknown Son
Fiancée for the Cameras

Born into Bollywood

Claiming His Bollywood Cinderella
The Surprise Bollywood Baby
The Secret She Kept in Bollywood

Signed, Sealed...Seduced

The Playboy's "I Do" Deal

Billion-Dollar Fairy Tales

Marriage Bargain with Her Brazilian Boss
The Reason for His Wife's Return
An Innocent's Deal with the Devil

The Powerful Skalas Twins

Saying "I Do" to the Wrong Greek
Twins to Tame Him

Visit the Author Profile page at Harlequin.com for more titles.

CONTRACTUALLY WED

TARA PAMMI

Harlequin
PRESENTS

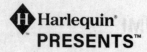

Harlequin® PRESENTS™

ISBN-13: 978-1-335-93932-6

Contractually Wed

Copyright © 2024 by Tara Pammi

 Harlequin Enterprises ULC
22 Adelaide St. West, 41st Floor
Toronto, Ontario M5H 4E3, Canada
www.Harlequin.com

Printed in Lithuania

Recycling programs for this product may not exist in your area.

CONTRACTUALLY WED

CHAPTER ONE

SNEAKING INTO THE Manhattan penthouse of the intensely private and vengeful Greek billionaire Apollo Galanis, a man she'd already annoyed a few times, at nine in the night, wasn't how Jia Shetty foresaw her twenty-sixth birthday evening going.

But given that no one had even remembered the date, much less celebrated it—not unusual either—it was the most excitement she'd seen on one. Though it was a panic-ridden *OMG what's he going to do to me when he finds me here?* kind of excitement rather than a belly-filled-with-butterflies kind.

Honestly, Jia had no idea how that kind of excitement tasted. Except maybe that one time when her rough sketches for the new wing of a billionaire's private library had been accepted. But only a flicker even then, because her family's well-being had depended on getting that contract. When her designs had been lauded innovative and environmentally intelligent, there had only been relief.

Because it hadn't been her name on the design, or her being praised for designing an architectural marvel. Tonight, her degree in architecture—only allowed by her father because Jia had shown talent for it and his own had long-ago deserted him—had come in handy as she planned to infiltrate Apollo Galanis's penthouse in a luxury hotel he himself had designed.

Whatever else the man soon to be her brother-in-law was, he was a brilliant architect, an innovator who believed in achieving more with less, a billionaire who was determined to leave the world better than he had found it.

Except for her family, that is.

Having studied the blueprints and worked as a cleaning lady for the past month at the hotel, Jia had finally figured out how to get into his penthouse. Learning the man's agenda for a given week wasn't that much of a stretch. From the moment he arrived in Manhattan, he demanded the presence of her older sister, Rina, his fiancée, like a master calling his prized poodle to attention.

Just thinking of her sister made panic tighten Jia's chest. Rina's tears last night as she'd sobbed with her head in Jia's lap that Apollo Galanis was a ruthless monster who expected her to sit, stand and perform at his command, had been playing in Jia's head in a loop.

How was her gentle, tenderhearted sister supposed to survive the strain of being Apollo Galanis's society wife if she couldn't even bear the stress of being his fiancée? How was Jia supposed to protect the only person in her life who had ever shown her kindness, if not by throwing herself as bait at the monster?

Relief hit her in waves as the key card she'd stolen from Galanis's designated maid worked on the digital menu and the elevator carried her away to the penthouse. She added another item to her increasing to-do list: make sure the maid didn't get into trouble for her actions.

The elevator opened with a swish and Jia stepped out, her eyes widening as she took in the architectural marvel of the penthouse.

Sweeping stairs made of wood and industrial metal straddled a palace-sized lounge with the ceiling stretching up to two levels. The ceiling and the walls were all glass, with load-bearing pillars breaking it up. Even those added to the modern industrial look of the space, fitting seamlessly into the concrete jungle around it. With the glittering lights of Manhattan and the sky itself open to the eye, it was as if one was standing in the midst of one of the most diverse cities in the world. As if one was both witness and a part of its constant reinvention of itself.

Other than a couple of turn-of-the-century art pieces in metal and wood again, the other adornment was lots of greenery. A giant fiddle-leaf fig and two monstera were the only plants Jia recognized among sturdier and more exotic greenery that warmed all the metal and wood, turning it into a much more intimate setting than the soulless chrome it could have been.

How could a man so eager and ruthless in his punishment of her family be the same one who had designed and given shape to this urban space full of such heart?

Jia knew she was violating his sacred space. He hadn't invited even her sister here. Maybe if Rina saw this, she would understand him a little better? But her older sister didn't have the same affinity that Jia had for old buildings and clean design lines. Neither was she as…worldly-wise as Jia was. Pampered and privileged and never having to doubt her parents' love for her. It was the first time life and their father were demanding something of Rina and she was simply crumpling against them.

In her case, life had forced Jia to learn to be tough, to understand that she had to provide value in any relationship.

Now Jia made a beeline to the kitchen, her stomach gnawing on itself. Munching on an apple, she looked through the state-of-the-art refrigerator that was big enough to hide in. Grabbing cheese and grapes and a wrapped bowl of what looked like pilaf with nuts, Jia spent the next few minutes trying to find the microwave hidden among the dark gray cabinets.

Finally, her pilaf was steaming, the grapes were cold and juicy, and the cheese perfectly crumbly as she reached the lounger that faced the Manhattan skyline.

Eating a meal with no one crying, losing their temper or conspiring in panic near her had become a luxury in the last few months. It also should have felt unnerving to sit in a space that belonged to the man who was turning their lives upside down.

Instead, Jia cherished the sweet tartness of the grapes and the buttery richness of the nutty pilaf. The cheese, she washed it down with a glass of chilled white wine and felt herself disappearing into the snug hold of the soft leather. Soon, she was snoring, her worries about selling herself to the devil all but forgotten.

Apollo Galanis walked into his Manhattan penthouse after a long, exhausting business trip to the Philippines and was in a sour mood since the property development deal there hadn't budged in two months.

His group of junior architects had made barely any changes to the designs he had already rejected. That they had the gall to invite him down there for another meeting pissed him off.

He'd wanted to fire the whole lot of them. Except these were the crème de la crème from the finest architecture programs across the world and if they didn't deliver, who would?

Neither could he fire them for something he himself was unable to deliver. He was blocked, or burned-out, or a bitter combination of both and he was beginning to see the reason.

It was this engagement he had talked himself into with the Shetty heiress. After more than a decade and a half of planning and strategizing and calculating ten moves ahead, he finally had Jay Shetty in his clutches.

The very man who had destroyed Apollo's father by stealing his designs and selling them as his own. His deepest trust betrayed, Papa had returned to Greece heartbroken and bankrupt, and had never recovered. Apollo was firmly planted on the board of directors of Jay Shetty's design company, with no way to gain controlling stock.

The older man, a conniving strategist, had shamelessly offered up his eldest daughter as a prize before Apollo could take even more drastic steps, like sending the man to prison. Jay's daughter would transfer her stock to Apollo after three years of marriage. It was clear that Jay was desperate to avoid other consequences Apollo could rain down on him. Was hoping to change Apollo's mind in three years.

The idea of reveling in Jay's desperation that Apollo might be sidetracked from revenge—a goal he'd pursued for nearly two decades—was immensely appealing. Giving the man a taste of the misery he'd brought on Apollo's family for years, by being present in his life as his son-in-law, by being the sword that was forever dangling over his head...sounded deliciously fitting.

Even though the last thing Apollo wanted was a wife.

One of the most beautiful women he'd ever seen, Rina Shetty was also demure, had acted as her father's society hostess for years, and was the kind of woman who would mold herself into whatever Apollo needed her to be.

Apollo had played into Jay's negotiation because Rina wasn't a bad choice for a wife for a man like him. A man who didn't believe in love and all that nonsense, a man who liked order and control in his every day, a man who would eventually need sons to carry on the legacy he was building. And really, who better than the grandchildren of the very man who had destroyed his family, to continue on the Galanis dynasty itself. There was a certain poetic justice in that.

Soon, Jay Shetty's company would be nothing but a speck absorbed into Galanis Corp, forgotten even by its own disgruntled, unhappy employees who were more than eager to prove their mettle and loyalty to the bigger, meaner predator that was circling their CEO.

And then maybe this hunger in him would appease, Apollo thought, with little faith in his own maybes. Maybe then, after nearly two decades, he could take a moment to celebrate everything he had achieved.

He took off his jacket, undid the buttons on his shirt, poured himself a glass of red wine and walked to his favorite lounger—the only piece of furniture he had restored and brought here from his home in Athens—to enjoy one of his two favorite views in the entire world.

Only to find it already occupied by a woman in a maid's uniform.

An empty white wine bottle sat on the floor next

to the lounger, along with a tray full of empty bowls and forks, all neatly stacked.

He had never invited even his mother or sisters to visit this particular project of his, and to find a member of staff not only breaking her professional code but invading his privacy, was untenable. He understood exhaustion and hard work but still…he paid exorbitantly well for his privacy.

Her white cap was on the floor, and the woman's gold-threaded dark brown hair fell in thick, lustrous waves, framing her familiarly angular face. He moved closer and turned on the Tiffany lamp, and let out a curse. Recognition came instantly and following it, *fury*.

Of course this was no maid transgressing his private space. This was a woman he had barely tolerated and he had known that the dislike was completely mutual.

In fact, in all of his thirty-nine years of life, Apollo had never met a woman, or even another person, who rubbed him the wrong way just by existing. Her mere presence had been like rubbing salt into a sunburn.

As if to provoke his ire even further, the sleeping woman let out a loud snore followed by an awful belch. Apollo had had enough. Before he could think better of the juvenile impulse, he was upending the glass of red in his hand over her head. At least it wasn't cold, he told himself.

She came awake, sputtering and squealing, unfolding like a mangy dog, and then mumbled something incoherent.

He grinned, wondering when he'd had so much fun in recent memory. Not even as a poor undergrad student at Harvard, or later when he'd made his first million, or even when he'd won environmental awards for his designs.

Finally, she stopped mumbling, rubbed her eyes and smeared the wine all over her face. Belatedly, Apollo realized he had just ruined his favorite lounger and the pristine carpet. *Christos*, not even a minute near her and she'd reduced him to a playground bully.

A grin appeared on her face even as she threaded her fingers through dark, wispy bangs that almost covered her eyes. "Just realized you ruined your own chair, did you?" she said, looking up at him, and running the tip of her tongue against that wide gap between her front teeth.

It was the first thing he had noticed about her—the imperfection of her crooked smile next to the pearly, near-perfect smile of her sister.

The differences between this woman's tall, boyish figure, with her thick glasses and thicker, untamed hair and her gap-toothed smile and her purple lipstick and her entire forearm covered in colorful tattoos and her skinny jeans and combat boots, against Rina's full, curvy figure, her polish and perfectly pitched tone when she spoke, her cream-colored jumpsuit, her hair neatly cut into blunt shoulder-length style, and a barely-there pink lip gloss on her lips, and the way she carried herself had nearly...had discombobulated him. Bringing into sharp contrast what he definitely didn't want in his life.

At the first meeting with Jay Shetty, his useless bag of a son, Rina and this...wild creature who sat next to her sister and asked impertinent questions, even as her father sent her dirty, shushing looks, Apollo had been unable to look away from her.

It was like watching a car crash, he had thought then. But two more meetings with her—where she was supposed to keep her sister company and where she had asked him too many intrusive, invading questions about what their married life was going to look like—Apollo had amended his first impression of her, begrudging it every inch of the way.

She was like a wild sunset, all splashy colors and a warm blaze.

And now when she grinned at him, not even a little effaced by the fact that he had caught her inside his private sanctuary, Apollo admitted what about her provoked him so much.

There was a rough, untamable kind of beauty to her, as if she had been born to be unleashed in the world to create a maximum kind of chaos. And he loathed chaos anywhere near him with a visceral re-action.

Still, even as he acknowledged that she equally attracted and repulsed him, he began to wonder why Jay had never offered her up as the proverbial lamb being led to slaughter. Why it had been his eldest he'd pushed toward Apollo.

"You have two minutes to explain why you're here, Ms. Shetty. Or it will be the jail for you. Not a big surprise that you will blend in very well with your…" he ran a hand over her form "…colorful persona."

Standing up, paying no heed to the fact that he was standing close and threatening her with prison, she grabbed a napkin from the tray and started dabbing at her uniform. Which only arrested his attention. The damned dress was short on her, barely covering her upper thighs. When she wrung the hem to get out an extra two drops of wine, it revealed the tops of her lacy tights hugging her lean, muscled thighs.

His gaze went up, noting the tight tuck of her waist and the two buttons that had come undone at her chest, revealing small breasts and gleaming golden-brown skin. The tail end of another tattoo snuck up under the collar of the dress, playing peekaboo with him.

Apollo looked away too late. Lust coursed through him like a sudden bolt of adrenaline shot into his very veins. He let out a shocked curse, something he never did in company, for it revealed too much of his state of mind. No, not this woman. *Christos.*

Lusting after his fiancée's sister…smacked too much of that wildness he disliked about this woman. Of being out of control.

Standing too close, she ran her tongue over her teeth. "You have to tell me which vintage that is," she said, making a rude, smacking noise. "As a rule, I don't drink reds since they give me horrible headaches. For that one, I might risk it. In fact, maybe you can just gift it to me, seeing that we're going to become close soon."

He gritted his teeth and prayed for a calm that felt out of reach. "Jail, Ms. Shetty."

"Fine," she said, her breath hitting him on a shuddering exhale.

Apollo knew he should step back, give his lungs air that was free of that lush red rose scent threaded with a twang of sweet sweat. But he didn't. He liked it too much and then there was the whole point of him backing away from her. Which he never would.

It was the latter mostly, he decided. She had invaded his home, showed little to no shame over it, and the last thing he was going to do was show her how much her presence…rattled him.

"Keep talking, Ms. Shetty."

"Okay, *sir*. Getting to it now, *sir*."

"Don't be ridiculous," he said, somehow controlling the urge to laugh out loud at her cheekiness. Or maybe drag her close and teach her some discipline if she was going to do that anyway. He closed his eyes, wondering why his mind was going to these strange, forbidden places, especially around this woman.

"If you insist on calling me Ms. Shetty in that tone, which by the way reminds me of my history professor, I have to call you that. My name's Jia. How come I've never heard you use it?"

"I have no need to become that...familiar with you."

"And yet, you have no problem getting all chummy with the rest of my family."

"They do not...provoke me like you do." He stepped farther into her space, which was his to begin with, forcing her to look up at him. Though it wasn't by much. She was taller than most women and he didn't have to look down at her as if from some great distance, and he liked this too. He wasn't supposed to like anything about this.

Something else struck him all of a sudden. He scowled. "How did you get in here? The security is infallible."

"And yet, here I am."

"You better start spewing answers to my questions, Ms. Shetty, or else..." He grinned, and opened the contacts list on his phone. "I have a feeling telling your father about your recent stunt is a better punishment than jail for you."

A soft, imperceptible shudder went through her and she stared at him, eyes wide. For once, that rough, *I can take on the world no matter what* attitude she wore like a second skin fell off, revealing the very young woman she was beneath. She looked at him as if he'd hit her below the belt. And damn if it didn't make him feel guilty. "I'm calling your bluff. You didn't squeal on me the last couple of times, *Apollo*," she said, making him feel foolish for the thirty seconds of guilt and curiosity he had felt for her.

Something about the way she drawled his name,

as if she'd said it in her head many times and with less sweetness than she used now, hit him in the pit of his stomach with a honey-like languor. "So you admit that it wasn't a mistake that Rina went to a different restaurant to meet me the first time, and that you nearly got tackled by my bodyguard the second time, and the third…time," he finally choked out on a swallowed laugh. Even he had found that third stunt enormously funny, with her using her brother's credit card that she'd filched from his jacket when she'd *accidentally* bumped into him and then gotten into trouble for making Jay Shetty's vein pop in his temple.

"Of course, I admit it. Not that I succeeded."

"What was the success criteria?" he said, suddenly curious.

"To make you despise our family enough that you'd leave Rina alone."

"And the recent episode where your sister burst into tears at the thought of moving to Athens with me?"

She flinched, as if she herself was in pain. "I wouldn't make her cry. Even to get rid of you." Then she brightened, "Wait! Clearly it put you off—"

"Not enough to break off the engagement. Rina, as your father explained, is gentle and completely overwhelmed by her good fortune."

The woman snorted. She actually snorted, probably spraying spittle onto his shirt.

Apollo refused to show, even by the twitch of his eyelid which was a hard thing to stop when he was pissed, that she was getting to him. "I assume that this...little stunt is to get my attention. So why don't you start with how you got in here in the first place?"

"I have been working at your hotel for the last month, cleaning suites. I studied the plans and figured out which elevator rides up here and the shifting schedule of your security. I made friends with the woman Sophia, the only one allowed to clean your penthouse. I stole her key card, got your schedule from Rina's phone and here I am." She said the last to some show tune he didn't recognize, her arms and hands gesticulating as if she were some great conductor.

He covered another step between them and now when that lush scent of hers wrapped around his body like a tendril of lust, he knew he was making a tremendous mistake. Still, he didn't back down.

Her big brown eyes widened and her shoulders trembled but she stubbornly stayed still. "Now that you've cost Sophia her job, tell me why you're here like an annoying pest."

"If you fire Sophia, I'll go to HR. I collected every document I could about how religiously on time she is, how many years she's worked here and how there hasn't been a single complaint about her. HR chose her for you because she hails from the same village as your father in Greece."

Apollo was struck speechless, having never met a worthier opponent. She had not only done her homework but she'd done it because she didn't want an innocent to get fired for her reckless act. Definitely not a trait he expected of Jay Shetty's progeny.

Another reason he'd thought Rina was perfect for him. She lacked personality and smarts and the kind of cunning that should be rampant in Shetty blood. This one had it in spades.

"What do you want?" he said, wanting nothing more than to get rid of her.

"I came here to make you a proposal."

"About?" he said, his heart suddenly pounding in his chest as if he were once again standing in line for an interview as a junior draftsman in a big architecture firm, nothing but dreams and goals in his wallet.

"An exchange of sorts. You release my sister from your engagement in return for…"

He waited, knowing that the flash of panic in her eyes was all too real. And yet like a predator hungry for a slice of flesh—her flesh—some unknown thing in his stomach grew. It wanted to eat up all her fear and taste the wildness writhing beneath. It wanted to pull away all that attitude, all those things she covered her skin in and reveal the real her to his gaze.

Seconds piled into minutes and the tip of her tongue flicked out to lick her wide lower lip. "In return for me," she said, her chest rising and falling. "I came here to sell you on the idea that I would make a far better wife to you than my sister." A harsh, self-deprecating laugh escaped her lips. "I broke into this maximum-security gilded cage, risked another woman's livelihood, risked more than your usual contempt, to sell myself to the devil. That's my evil plan."

CHAPTER TWO

CALLING HIM THE devil was probably not the best way to convince Apollo Galanis that she was a better prospect than her sister but then when had Jia's plans ever gone according to script? Her entire life, including her conception into this world, had been ruled by Murphy's Law.

This brilliant scheme to impress her sister's fiancé with her smarts and cunning and guts had looked different in her head. He was a ruthless, ambitious billionaire who was determined to cut her father's small architecture firm into pieces. She'd convinced herself that a man like that would appreciate her taking this initiative.

Of course, she'd fallen asleep in his favorite lounger. And now as he watched her with those intense gray eyes, she realized what she'd left out in her calculations and it was a biggie.

Apollo Galanis was not some manageable, ordinary man she kept reducing him to in her head. It was both delusional and dangerous.

There had been this…sparkling, tense energy between them from the first moment. She'd pretended to be her sister, Rina, and chatted away about her intense and scorching sex life, hoping to put him off, while he had known that she wasn't Rina and played along.

At the end, after she'd made a flaming fool of herself by comprehensively describing the foursome she'd just walked out of, his mouth had twitched and her gaze had gone to the sudden, blinding beauty of his lips and he'd caught her watching and that had been that.

Since then, as much as Jia had tried to fill the space between them with her loathing of him and he with his contempt for her, there had been something more volatile in the mix. Something she had refused to acknowledge in the beginning, something that had kept her awake later, the very something that had finally led to this madcap plan. That the basis of her proposal was "this energy" between them made her face and neck hot, even with her skin damp and sticky.

At least, he hadn't laughed at her.

But as the seconds and his silence stretched, being laughed at felt better than his scrutiny.

"Show me your skills, then. Sell yourself to me," he said, walking away.

Jia blinked as bright lights came on, her body suddenly flush with humming energy, her brain chugging along painfully slow to the fact that he wasn't throwing her out.

When she turned around, he was sitting on the white leather couch, one arm spread out over the back of it, one leg over the other, his expression one of smooth, wicked humor that Jia wanted to slap off his face. He looked like he was the lord of something, *everything*, and she, a poor peasant come to present her pathetic case.

"I'm waiting. Clearly, you think yourself a better candidate than your sister. Sell me on it."

If his gaze had moved down her neck in that condescending way of his, that told her she was nothing but amusing entertainment, she might have lost it. Instead, he looked at her with that conviction that nothing, *nothing*, in the world could convince him to take her on.

And that…that arrogance filled her with renewed resolve. All her life, she had known little kindness and love and the little she had, had come from her sister. She'd do anything to stop Rina's ruin at his hands. Even if it meant courting her own.

"My sister is gentle, kind and…in love with our ex-con chauffeur. As heartless as you are, I'm assuming you would hate a woman whose affections for you are in doubt."

"Your sister's too nice to cheat on me once we're married and too gentle, just like you said, to give her marriage vows anything but full commitment. As for affections, those are fickle and I have no use for them."

Jia's mouth fell open.

"That's what you based this whole escapade on?" he said, mouth twitching.

"Partly, yes," Jia said, refusing to let him get to her. "I mean, I knew you were a ruthless, unemotional robot but hearing the proof from your own mouth…" She made a show of ticking off an item on her imaginary checklist. "I also took a little nice detour down your dating history on the good old web and from all the women you've dated—kudos to the diversity in your playing ground BTW—it's clear—"

"BTW?"

"By the way," she said, sighing. "Moving on, it's clear that you like bold, adventurous, dare I say, even ballsy women for your…partners. Rina's nothing like them. She won't even fight back if you…"

"Careful, Ms. Shetty. Just because I let you insult me doesn't mean you can attribute weaknesses to my character."

"You'll be bored within two days. Why are you so intent on having the most boring marriage in the world?"

"Boring marriages last."

"Wow, so you're really only going for quantity, not quality?"

"I still haven't heard one word about how you're a better candidate. Only disparagement of your sister."

She gasped, feeling outraged. "I'm trying to protect Rina and you from—"

"Tell me," he said, leaning forward, for the first time showing a sliver of curiosity. "Did Rina ask you to save her from this predicament or is this all an elaborately spun lie so that you could have me for yourself?"

"Of course she asked me. Like multiple times. In fact, she's been…" Jia let out an angry breath, realizing the blasted man had tricked her into admitting it.

Something almost like distaste curled his upper lip. But then, his lips always seemed to greet the world with that lick of contempt. "Look, my sister is…" she began, wanting to defend Rina but he raised a hand.

She was so shocked he was engaging in dialogue that her brain stupidly followed his commands. "Why are you a better bet? You and I both know you have something bigger for you to drop."

Jia shouldn't have been surprised that he had figured her out. But she couldn't play her ace just yet. "You and I have chemistry. And your plan to punish my father would yield a thousand percent more results if it was me you—"

He shot to his feet and moved toward her, and Jia's synapses gave out. That lizard part of her brain seemed to come awake, screaming, *Hot sexy man at twelve o'clock.*

She craned her neck, just slightly, to look up into his face when he left only a foot or so between them. God, he smelled like cinnamon and pine and reminded her of decadent winter evenings spent near her mom's feet while she knitted.

This close, she could see the lines of tiredness fanning out from Apollo's eyes. And even as it reduced him from that larger-than-life figure in her head, Jia didn't like seeing them. Didn't like knowing him at this level.

"That's an interesting observation. Care to prove it?"

"Prove it…how?" she said, her throat suddenly dry, and hating herself for taking a step back. She should have known the beast would play with her.

"Kiss me. Then we will know if you're really a better proposition than—"

She pressed her hand to his mouth. Something hot and feral came awake in his gray eyes, something she hadn't even been sure he was capable of feeling.

"Please don't—"

"You should know, Jia," he said, wrapping long fingers around her wrist and tugging her hand away from his mouth. "Every game you begin, I will play, and play to win."

Her name on his lips was a sweet threat. A reminder that she was playing a dangerous game, that she was letting this attraction go to her head. And maybe even handing him a weapon. And he was right. He was a master at this. "Fine. I'll show you my ace. But you have to promise that you'll grant me three wishes in the aftermath. Whatever I ask for."

"You're so sure you'll win me over?"

"Give me your word, Apollo. Three conditions for our deal in your language."

"How do you know I won't go back on them?"

"Because I just know," she said, hating the fact that she trusted him. How had that happened?

That little flicker of heat again in his eyes and then a nod.

Jia drew in a deep breath, even as fear spread its tentacles wide and far in her body. If she did this, there was no turning back. If she did this, she was tying her future—at least half a decade in the best-case scenario—to this man, who was bent on ruining her family. If she did this, her father was never going to give her what she'd desperately craved for years.

But it was the only way to protect Rina and the only way to stop her father from getting hurt by this man who would not hesitate when he discovered her father's lies. And while the thought of settling into unholy matrimony, even for a temporary period, with this man turned her inside out, it would at least serve as a break from her own life. Especially if Rina summoned the courage to stand up to their father and leave home.

"The plans for the new wing of that private library in Seattle, the low-income apartments out in Brooklyn, my brother, Vik…didn't design any of that stuff."

"It's his name on the blueprints," Apollo said, thunder in his eyes. "He accepted a bloody award for it. His face was on a magazine cover for…who? Who's the architect?"

"Me. I drew the initial plans. And the revisions after you requested them. And… I did all of them. So, there you have it. I'm the asset you want. You take me out of Dad's company and…it loses its prestige faster than you can cut it up. It won't win any more contacts moving forward." Something thick and sticky coated her throat and Jia had to swallow to speak past it. "You marry me, and take me away from the company, and you truly have won."

Apollo took one look into those big, brown eyes, saw the tears she blinked away in a quick flash and knew she was telling the truth. Fury gripped him, even as his usual rationale tried to wrangle it into control.

He shouldn't be surprised by further proof of Jay Shetty's duplicitous nature. Suddenly, all of the older man's attempts to keep his younger daughter away from Apollo made sense. He had assumed Jay was attached to Jia and he'd had no interest in the woman with her rough edges and vulgar stories and her constant attempts to draw him into a fight.

Now he realized how perfectly Jay had played him by dangling his beautiful, perfect, dull-as-cardboard firstborn in front of Apollo. But why rob his own daughter of her name and her accolades...why pass it on as his son's talent...?

"You studied architecture. Your brother on the other hand was thrown out of college," he said, having cast a cursory glance at her records when the PI he'd hired had dug up everything on the Shetty family.

Usually, he would never overlook the details just because it was a woman. But from the first moment she'd walked into the restaurant pretending to be her sister and let herself loose on him, Apollo had decided that she was of no significance to him, that she was no more than a buzzing fly.

She shrugged, her mouth clamped, all of that dark humor and the teasing taunts gone. Her admission had clearly come at a high price and she'd still done it.

Her claim was that she wanted to save her sister from the horrible fate of being married to him? But why put herself in his sights, then? Nothing about Jia Shetty made sense to his logical brain.

"Is this another game your father's playing?" he said, his voice full of irritation at himself.

She went to sit on the couch. Tucking her feet under her knees, she leaned back and let out a loud exhale. The maid uniform rode up on her thighs, revealing smooth skin on top of the stockings and another button popped on the bodice, revealing the curve of a breast. She thrummed with an artless sensuality he found irresistible. "He's going to hate me for spilling the family's dirty secret." He heard the slight quiver in her words. "You can be sure of that."

"Why are you going against your own family, then? Or is lack of loyalty a family trait, passed down in blood?"

Her bow-shaped lips flinched. "My father is playing a foolish game, thinking he can change your mind in three years. Thinking he can impress you with my talent at the helm. He doesn't realize how many things could be ruined by continuing this…feud. I'm trying to save everyone."

"Why?"

"What do you mean, why? You're here, having maneuvered yourself onto the board, because my father stole something from yours more than two decades ago, aren't you?"

"Not a small something," Apollo said, gritting his jaw. The die was cast and yet some part of him wanted to understand her. "Your family doesn't deserve—"

"That's my decision."

She looked up at him as he moved toward her, the lamplight throwing the long line of her neck into relief. Everything about her was achingly lovely, perfection stitched together painfully with a multitude of imperfections.

He should turn away from her and her proposal, turn back on the entire idea of ruining Jay Shetty, and yet, Apollo had never been so aroused, his interest engaged on many levels. Everything about her was a challenge, a lure and a promise and the extreme achiever in him wanted to unravel her on every level. And conquer her.

"Maybe all this is a scheme to tie you to myself?" She let out a throaty laugh, and the collar of her uniform shifted to reveal a little more of her tattoo. "Maybe I'm stealing you from Rina because of my uncontrollable lust for you?"

For all her flippant taunts, she stiffened when he sat down on the coffee table in front of her, caging her between his legs. Elbows on his knees, he leaned forward until he could see the browns of her eyes widen into large pools.

"What are your conditions?"

Her soft gasp was a whistle through the gap between those front teeth, tiny beads of sweat over her bow-shaped upper lip. It took her several more breaths to focus on his words and he suppressed a smile at that. Maybe the lust thing wasn't just a bluff. Her gaze met his finally, a steely resolve in it. "You will not retaliate against my father for this."

"And?"

"You will divorce me after two years, after you've exploited everything you can out of me."

"I intend to marry only once in my life, Tornado," he said, making it crystal clear that he wasn't giving her up. Not when he was just discovering what a treasure she was on multiple levels. "Whether that's your spineless sister or prickly you, I will make it work. I'll relish your father's—"

"I'm already aware of your elaborate revenge scheme. But believe me, you aren't going to want me anywhere near you in a year, tops. I'm generously granting you two."

He didn't hide his smile then. And when her gaze skidded to his mouth with a near-comical helplessness, he felt punch-drunk with desire. "No."

"You promised," she said, almost stomping those combat boots on the floor, in something akin to a tantrum.

He raised a brow, thoroughly unsure of what to make of this woman-child creature. If his assessment of those designs was right, and he was always right, she was not only brilliant but innovative in her field at a young age. There was the fact that she was writing her life away into the enemy's hands to protect her undeserving family. Then this…outward toughness she projected—from how she dressed to how she talked and acted—then there was the quicksilver flash of fear coursing through her body and her trust in him. And he felt as if he was standing at the door of either his biggest victory or his doom. The excitement in his blood though, the sudden hum in his veins…it seemed to not care.

"You should have specified that it was about the marriage itself."

"Ugh, you're…"

"You think I can't tolerate you, *ne*?" he said, softening without wanting to or seeming like he was. "Leave it to time."

"Fine."

"You'll be expected to spend a little time in Greece every year," he said, purposefully making it vague.

Apprehension filled her eyes.

"Is that a problem, Jia?" he asked softly, pressing down hard on his curiosity. Now that he had her, a true asset if he'd ever known one, nearly locked up, he didn't want to spook her.

"My entire life is in New York."

"But you're willing to give it up for Rina, no? And to be honest, it doesn't look like much of a life to me."

"You don't know anything about me," she said, the protest without fire.

Instantly, he felt the need to soothe her, for more than the obvious reason. "And your last condition for me?"

"Oh, I'm saving that one for later. It's more in the lines of a wedding present," she said, feathery eyebrows wriggling up and down.

Apollo felt the most insane urge to grab her and kiss the insouciance out of her. He wanted to reduce her to nothing but sounds and gasps, to wrest some kind of control from her, to prove to himself that she and her sister were interchangeable.

Christos, the thought of a kiss had never aroused or riled him so.

When he didn't say anything, she stood up, even though there was little space between his legs. "The wedding," she said, looking down at him now, "has to be a quiet, city hall affair. I can do Thursday and—"

He shot to his feet too. "No, absolutely not."

They were standing close enough that her chest grazed his just so. "This is an arrangement, a boardroom deal. Do we have to dress it up as some big romantic affair?"

"Yes."

"Fine. Don't blame me if I disappear the day before the wedding and you find Rina walking toward you."

"Are you planning to?"

"My family isn't going to be happy about this. Not just *not happy*. They might do anything to stop me."

"Because you're your father's golden goose," he finished, finally understanding her point. She seemed to have no illusions about her value to them. And yet, every time she talked about them, something sad and desperate filled her eyes.

"And I come with the same stock options as Rina. You can have them after two years of blissfully wedded life."

Apollo had never sought to punish the man's children for his sins. Marrying Rina after Jay had dangled the stock in his face, especially after he'd discovered that she had the spine of a noodle and would serve well as a wife, had been simply another step toward his goal. But with this woman, it felt like she was turning herself into a willing victim for her family.

It left a bitter taste at the back of his throat.

She waved her phone in his face, the action and her general irreverence and her body language all nearly alien to him. "Text me when you have the license."

"I have the license. Only the name needs to be changed."

She pressed a palm to her chest, her eyelashes fluttering. "Oh, how romantic."

Just as she bypassed him, Apollo reached for her. She fell into him with a soft oomph, her thighs pressing into his. "I have agreed to all your conditions, *ne*? I have one too."

"I'm not giving you any more dirt on my father."

He grinned then and cupped her cheek slowly. "What a diabolical mind you have, Jia. I have something more personal in mind."

Her eyelashes fluttered rapidly, like butterfly wings, and her lips too. "What?"

"All this chemistry you claim there is between us, this uncontrollable lust you have for me... I would like a taste of it. After all, I switched my choice to you pretty fast. I need a reminder as to why."

"Why? You didn't kiss Rina after all."

He grinned. "And how would you know if I kissed your sister or not?"

Color rose to her too-sharp cheeks and she shrugged. But she didn't shy her gaze away. "I... asked her."

"Why, Jia?"

Her gaze flicked to his mouth like a liquid caress, going straight to his groin. "Every time I saw you together, it was like pairing a wolf with an adorable baby chick. I kept waiting for you to realize she was too sweet and good and docile for you, and I was... curious about how a man could burn up for one sister and kiss the other. So I asked her, again and again."

"I was burning up for you? Your confidence is interesting, if nothing else."

"It's a fact."

"That your attraction to me is real," he said, satisfaction strumming through him like an unchecked river.

"Yes," she said, an edge of defensiveness to the word. "It's chemistry. I won't be made to feel shame over it."

He wondered who had made her feel shame over

it and how he could reduce them to ash. "I am beginning to see one big advantage to this union, then. And getting quite excited about it too."

Her gaze flicked to his crotch and then back up. *Christos*, the woman was bold. "You sure your...hard-on isn't because of what I can do for you?"

He threw his head back and laughed, true enjoyment coursing through him. And her eyes on him, tracking everything, drinking everything in...was a shot of desire injected straight into his veins. "I do believe we have one thing in common, Jia. Refusing to believe in delusions."

"So admit the truth, then. Power is the thing that gets you off."

"In this case, no. I should very much like to fuck you, as soon as possible. Is that clear enough?"

Her only reaction was the slight widening of her eyes and the heavy rise and fall of her chest. "Pleasure before World Domination for Apollo Galanis? That's...an unexpected turn."

"Well, you are quite the package."

"If we do this..." she said, her palm coming to rest on his chest with a boldness that set his muscles to curl with need "...if you really want us to have an actual marriage with sex and all that, for however long it lasts, you have to get rid of your other...girlfriends or flings or whatever you call them. You have to get rid of Portia Wentworth, like tonight." Her palm slammed into his chest in emphasis, his latest convenient partner's name gritted out. "I won't share you, even if you're not actually mine in the true sense…"

Apollo caught her mouth with his, her fierce claim as much of an aphrodisiac as the rough pants of her breaths. She was midsentence and her mouth was open and he swooped in, his want as raw and visceral as he'd ever known it to be. *Dios mio*, her lips were incredibly soft and she tasted sweet and tart.

She made a soft sound into his mouth, both complaining and eager, when he grazed her lower lip with his teeth, didn't back away. If anything, her fingers wound tighter around his neck and she leaned into him a little more.

Apollo pulled her closer, the dip of her waist and the flare of her hips as he moved his hands lower a lush invitation. He grabbed her bottom, deepening the kiss. She pushed onto her toes and bit his lip. A rough groan escaped him, as her belly rubbed against his hard shaft. *Christos*, he couldn't wait to taste her everywhere, couldn't wait to reduce her to nothing but his name and her pleasure at his hands.

After what felt like no more than a few seconds, he pulled back, eager to see lust paint its fingers over her sharp features. Still clinging to him, Jia buried her face in his neck, in a gesture that made him feel… something. Her little hot pants pinging over his skin like music notes.

Then she was pulling away, running her palm over her belly, her chest rising and falling, her gaze rapidly scanning everything around them but barely touching his.

Arms folded, amused despite the deafening thud of desire in his blood, Apollo watched her with growing fascination. The woman was a puzzle and a present wrapped in one and he couldn't wait to unwrap her *and* unravel her.

She collected her cap, her handbag that had fallen under the lounger, and after what felt like an eternity, faced him. Brown eyes danced with lust-heavy brightness. "So this is on?"

He grinned, tucking his hands in his trouser pockets to stop himself from reaching for her again. "Are you waiting for a romantic proposal?"

She made a face at him but there was something very practiced about it. Apollo wondered at how much of her toughness was armor and what it hid. "Given I proposed to you, that will just be another farce, no? At least, we have a good story to tell when it all burns down."

He refused to argue the point with her. "There will be a car downstairs to take you home. It's past eleven."

She looked surprised. "Don't need it. I'm used to taking care of myself."

"And I'm used to taking very good care of my assets," he said, without missing a beat.

Her shoulders rounded, even as she gave him a two-fingered salute. "Of course you do."

Standing in the empty lounge, Apollo stared after

the elevator doors, twin pulses of excitement and unease knotting in his stomach. More emotion than he had felt in a long, long time.

CHAPTER THREE

A WEEK LATER, as he arrived at the Shetty mansion—
an ugly showboat if he'd ever seen one, jutting out
amidst the surrounding dense, thick woods like a sore
thumb—Apollo could not believe that he had been
married for two days.

He *was* actually married and it had only registered
when he'd given the news to his mother. After years
of begging/threatening him to marry and have a life
outside of his work, she had been delighted.

Until he had told her that he had married the daughter of the man who had ruined her husband, who had
broken their family in ways they hadn't healed from.

But Mama was too gracious to voice her dislike.
His sisters had jumped on the call and complained
that he had deprived them of a celebration. It had been
months since he'd returned to Greece, so he promised to bring his wife home and let his sisters throw
them a grand reception.

His wife, Jia.

He couldn't help testing the fit and shape of those
words on his lips, couldn't help the flare of intense

satisfaction of such a complex woman bearing his name.

He wondered if the novelty of her numerous edges and contours would be enough to keep his interest aflame for an entire lifetime. Like showing up at the Manhattan city hall for their civil wedding in a lacy white silk tank top without a bra and skinny black jeans and fuchsia-colored stiletto heels.

With tiny diamond studs at her ears and dark red lipstick her only adornment. The thick, wavy strands of her gold-burnished brown hair had been hanging loose to her waist.

She had looked sensational and stunning and sensual enough that men turned to stare as she walked toward him. He had spied a thin, fragile gold chain when she'd neared him, a single, tiny sapphire pendant shimmering against her golden-brown skin. And as she played with it, turning it round and round while they signed the forms, Apollo knew that it was a talisman.

She had so bravely caught his interest away from her sister, achieved her goal, openly admitting to being attracted to him, laid down conditions for this marriage, and yet, she was nervous and alone and so...painfully young.

The whole time until the registrar announced they were married and they walked into the October sunshine, she had been waiting for someone. When he inquired, she made a show of looking like she didn't care. Then she admitted that Rina had said she might come.

Tenderness and something more twisted through Apollo, emotions he didn't want to feel, especially for his new bride. He still wasn't sure of her motives, and he didn't want to forget she was her father's daughter.

She was an important acquisition. And he did need her healthy and functioning for the next part of his plan to come to fruition. Feeling uncharacteristically indulgent, he'd asked her where she wanted to have their wedding breakfast. And she, of the infinite surprises, had demanded a pretzel from a street cart.

Contrary to his expectations, he'd enjoyed the salty, buttery pretzel, chased by a grape soda and then, her lips stained purple from the sugary drink, the tip of her nose pink in the cold, she'd asked him if he intended to kiss her again, with noisy New Yorkers flowing around them without breaking stride.

Apollo had broken his natural distaste for PDA and kissed her. She had tasted like salt and sugar and everything in between. It was a miracle he had been able to break away from her, instead of dragging her up to his penthouse and ravishing her to his heart's content.

He was absolutely going to enjoy the passion simmering between them but he wouldn't let it control him, couldn't let his fascination with her distract him from almost two decades' worth of planning.

And now, two days later—more than enough time for her to have broken the news to her family—her silence was beginning to weigh on him. He was breaking his promise to her that he'd let her spend another month on this side of the pond, but after three unanswered calls to her cellphone, after she'd promised him to be available, and this strange unease in his gut, he'd had enough.

It was time to collect his asset.

He got out of his chauffeured car to find the illustrious Shetty family sitting out on the lawn, looking as if they were posing for a photoshoot featuring one of America's richest families.

Except Jia.

Something about the picture bothered Apollo and it had been the same every time. Either Jia usually ran around taking care of logistics or stood outside the circle the other three formed.

Rina got to her feet as Apollo neared them, as did her father, though a bit slower. Her brother, Vik, lounged in his chair, his legs spread out far and wide—all useless posturing. Apollo had instantly disliked him at the first meeting six months ago. Now, knowing that he had willingly passed off Jia's hard work and talent as his own, his assessment was spot-on.

"Where is she?"

Rina paled at his tone while Jay's mouth flattened. "You had no right to turn her head. My lawyer's preparing annulment papers even as we speak and if I were you—"

"But I would never be you, Jay," Apollo bit out

softly. "I would never steal intellectual property from a man I called friend and benefit from it while his family struggled. Apparently, stealing IP and passing it on as one's own is a family trait."

A paleness emerged beneath his skin. Hurriedly, Jay threw out an arm to stop his son, who'd shot to his feet.

"I could have you both in prison in an hour for IP theft. But Jia, probably the smartest of you lot, made a deal with me. As for an annulment, there will be no cause for that after today."

The man flushed a deep red.

"Where is she?" Apollo repeated.

"She's…unwell, Mr. Galanis," Rina said, "or she—"

"So unwell that she couldn't answer the phone? Or is she saving one of you from another mess?"

Rina blanched. "It's just that—"

"Already missing me, darling?" came a soft, husky voice from behind him.

Apollo turned to find his new bride a few feet away, dressed in a black lace top and black jeans, her hair in a messy bun on top of her head, her expressive eyes hidden behind wraparound shades.

Whatever unease he had felt didn't dissolve at seeing her. If anything, it intensified. Reaching her, he snatched the shades off her face. A deep, black-and-blue bruise shone under her left eye, stretching sideways toward her cheekbone where she had two butterfly stitches.

Rage swept through him. Was this the reason she

had so readily made a deal with him? To escape from this?

Her eyes flared with apprehension at whatever she saw in his face and she took a step back. It was enough for Apollo to steady himself. One hand on her hip, he gently pulled her closer. Something in him calmed when she came without protest.

He ran the pad of his thumb under the bruise, careful not to touch the painful-looking boundary against unmarred skin. "What happened?" he said softly, loathing the presence of their audience, wishing he had never let her come back here.

"I tripped and landed my cheek on the leg of a table."

"Hmm...right after we got married too," he said, not missing the practiced, neat explanation. "This is the reason you wouldn't answer my calls?"

"Rina took me to the ER and it took forever. I had to get stitches and then I had the worst headache for hours. I popped a couple of sleeping pills and slept for, like, twenty hours straight."

Apollo didn't push it, even though she wasn't telling him the complete truth. One of the two men behind him were responsible for her bruise. If he pushed her, she would only double down on her lie. And he wanted her to trust him. "Why didn't you text me?"

"I didn't realize my phone battery had died. This morning, you kept video calling me." She made a tsking sound, leaning closer. Her fingers played with the buttons of his shirt, and every swipe of her fingertip against his throat tightened the knot of desire in his gut. "The last thing I wanted was my new husband to see what a frightful sight I was and return the merchandise. I was feeling sad enough that I didn't get a proper wedding night."

Despite his simmering rage, Apollo's mouth twitched. There was something almost adorable when she put on that hot-for-him act. He couldn't wait to discover how much of it was real. "You're a horrible flirt. Fortunately for me," he said, just to tease her.

"Hey! You're just not used to women coming on to you freely, are you? My generation believes in owning our desires. I foresee a lot of this age gap causing problems in our married life," she finished with a sigh. "It could count as 'irreconcilable differences' when we—"

Apollo shut her up the only way he knew, and the only way he wanted to. He caught her mouth with his, and she was surprised enough that she gasped.

It was their third kiss and the fact that he was keeping count like a teenager betrayed more than he cared to admit. But not enough to stop him from deepening it when she opened up with a soft moan. *Christos*, she was sweet and hot and he was regretting not taking her back to the penthouse immediately after their wedding. Her father wouldn't be threatening him with annulment and he would have had the chance to explore this fizzing need and bring it under control.

He gentled himself when she panted, even as his arousal heightened by the weight of her pressed up against him. For all her outward toughness, she was a skinny, almost fragile thing in his hands. Her fingers fluttered over his jaw and instantly, the kiss changed tenor, became softer, sweeter, as if she could magic out of it what she needed.

When she pulled back with another soft sigh and hid her face in his chest, Apollo wrapped his arms around her in what he would call a tender embrace. Which was another first for him because he wasn't the man women flocked to for tenderness and understanding.

Her tight knuckles drummed against his chest as she looked up. He saw a flash of anger in her eyes, directed at herself and him, before she cursed. She hadn't wanted that kiss to happen in front of her family.

Because she'd painted a picture of the suffering in store for her as his wife? Or because she felt exposed at her clear attraction to the family's enemy? Or because she had a whole new scheme cooking in her cunning brain and he'd disturbed it by showing up ahead of time?

Dios mio, the sooner he took her out of this place and from among them, the better for both of them. He could stop feeling like a caged animal at the mercy of its base desires and return to the rationality he knew and needed.

He rubbed his palm over her back, marveling at the wiry, lean strength of her body. Marveling at his attraction to a woman who was such a study in contrasts. "Say goodbye. We're leaving. Now."

She looked up, confusion clouding her sparkling brown eyes. "Now? You said I had six weeks."

"I didn't realize that you needed a keeper."

She stiffened, reminding him of his older sister's cat. "It's an accident, Apollo. Just a bruise."

"Do you really want to get into what it is now, *matia mou*?"

Her mouth turned down at the corners. "Give me at least until tonight."

"You have fifteen minutes and it's more than enough to collect your various electronics."

She pushed back from him then, mistrust shining in her eyes. "Not to say a proper goodbye and it's—"

"Now, Jia," he said, letting her see the temper he was tamping down. "Before I forget all my promises or that I still owe you one."

She straightened, shutting down whatever little vulnerability she had shown him. "If I'm using that one, it can't be half-assed."

He regarded her with an outside calm, even as he knew what she would ask. "What's the full condition, then?"

"I don't want to talk about this ever again."

He didn't need to ask her what she meant. He didn't give his assent nor did she ask for confirmation. If she trusted him that much already, that was her problem. But no way was she getting what she wanted this time.

She belonged to him and he would destroy the man who had lifted a hand against her, whoever it was.

All through the flight to Athens, Jia kept wishing her husband was truly the closed-off, ruthless monster she'd made him out to be in her head all these months. A villain full of nefarious intentions and cutthroat tactics could have served her so much better.

His calling her his "asset," his telling her father that there would be no annulment after tonight, his demand that she leave instantly at his command… all of it pricked like a thorn stuck under her skin. But it was no less than what she'd expected. He was a powerful man used to getting his way and she was an important pawn.

Just because he'd gotten angry over her bruise, or kissed like he meant to soothe her…didn't mean much. The fortunate thing was that all her life, beginning very early on, she'd had a taste of everything but real love. Oh, her older sister, Rina, had been kind to her and loved her—even when it invited their father's annoyance—but it was the same emotion that she showed a puppy that Vik had tormented when they'd been kids.

Her father's begrudging acknowledgment and a little affection had come *after* she began showing real talent in architecture, after she'd won several contracts for the company, *after* she had repaid his generosity in letting her mother keep her.

Until then she'd been only a reminder of his wife's infidelity.

So Jia knew not to mistake Apollo's rage at her bruise for anything more than basic human decency, or his concern as anything more than another reason to hate her family. His demand that she leave her family behind was nothing but his need to make sure "their deal" was completed ASAP.

She was a willing pawn at worst, and an important asset at best. And in between, a weapon to be used against her father. Hopefully, her actions would count toward nullifying the last. Of course, her father had been furious, muttering that she'd ruined everything, ranting about an annulment.

Now, as she whiled away the hours on the jet, sitting across from Apollo, with a low buzzing ache at the back of her head that wouldn't let her sleep, Jia wished she could enjoy the flight. Wished she could ignore him as easily as he was ignoring her.

Through the drive to the private airstrip and the two hours into the flight so far, he'd barely looked at her, his dark mood hanging over the luxurious space like a thunderous cloud.

"Do you need medical attention, Jia?"

Jia sat up at the sudden question. Every time he said her name, it felt like a caress and a reprimand rolled into one. And while she wasn't going to go out of her way to please him, she didn't understand his animosity. She'd handed him everything he'd wanted on a platter without making any demands. What was his problem?

"I'm perfectly fine," she said, flicking an imaginary dust mote from her jeans. Clearly, he had been watching her the whole time.

"You keep rubbing your head and your neck."

"I'm a little out of sorts," she snapped and sighed. "You did drag me away from my family and my things and…"

"Your precious collection of lacy silk blouses and dark denim?"

"Exactly," she said, not letting the smile that wanted to bloom touch her lips. He wasn't allowed to be grumpy one second and then charm her the next.

He stood up and before she could take in a rushed breath, loomed over her, filling her field of vision. With his shirt unbuttoned to reveal olive skin at his throat, his corded forearms sprinkled with hair and his gray eyes focused on her…he was incredibly intimidating, to say the least.

She'd been confident they would lead separate lives for most of the year. Given he traveled a lot and would want her to continue her work for the family firm. She hadn't expected to be around him so much so soon.

Something about him made her feel unbalanced. Which was why she'd played offense and admitted her attraction to him. Better to own it than let him turn it into a weapon.

He extended his hand toward her and that bubble of tension around them tightened. "Come."

After staring at it for a few seconds, she placed her hand in his with a tremble she couldn't hide. He pulled her up and shuffled them toward the rear cabin, telling the flight attendant that they weren't to be disturbed.

Jia flushed at the idea of the entire flight knowing what they were up to, and when dampness bloomed between her thighs, she flushed a little more. God, a one-word command from him and she was melting like an ice cream cone on a summer day.

You told yourself you'd enjoy this, remember, a voice whispered and she scoffed. She had done that. Out of this whole miserable deal—for which one party hated her and the other didn't trust her—hot, fun sex with the sexiest man she'd ever known was the one highlight she'd imagined could happen.

Theory was one thing and reality a whole other.

She was trembling by the time he closed the privacy curtains on them. What if she didn't please him? What if he was…?

"Take off your clothes," he said, once they were inside the luxurious rear cabin.

"What?" she said, whispering the word past the deafening pounding in her ears.

"Your clothes, I want them off. Do you need help?"

A sliver of mockery had crept into his voice and it made her spine straighten. That little twitch at the corner of his mouth…it reduced him to earthly dimension, made him look deceptively adorable.

Rolling her shoulders back in a conscious movement, Jia shook her head. "No, I don't."

She licked her lips, searching for a reason to ask for the lights to be dimmed or to just put this off for now. The twinkle in his eyes said he was expecting her to do just that and damned if she was going to let him box her like that.

"I thought you were very excited for all the sex we were going to have," he added, sitting down at the edge of the bed and loosely caging her between his legs. With his hands pressing into the bed, head tilted up, he looked like an emperor assessing his latest gift. "Don't tell me all of that was a pretense to trap me."

Jia's heart gave a thud against her rib cage. "Of course not," she said, swallowing past a swarm of butterflies in her throat. It was so much easier to make bold statements than actually be bold in front of him in such an intimate setting. "But I was expecting some foreplay at least."

"My eyes on you won't turn you on?"

Heat streaked her cheeks. "I don't know," she said, opting not to lie.

"You're of the generation that likes to try everything, *ne*? So let's see if stripping for me does anything for you."

Her mouth twitched at how cleverly he used her own words against her. She played with the lacy hem of her tank top, without meaning to be coy. His gaze slid there and away. "And you? Ordering me around turns you on?"

He grinned then, and somehow it felt more real than anything she'd seen in his expressions. As if she'd caught him by surprise once again and he liked that. A lot. "Not simply ordering you, Jia. But seeing you fight the instinct to give in definitely turns me on. It's quite…alluring."

How easily he read her…

He raised a brow, his arctic gray eyes sparkling. "But I don't want to develop a reputation as a miserly husband. I'll give you as much foreplay as you need, if this doesn't work."

Jia took her blouse off and then shimmied out of her jeans, which was quite the feat with him looking on, because they were tight and she wasn't full of grace, like him. She stood in front of him in a strapless bra that pushed her small breasts up and matching panties in blush pink, her pulse going haywire all through her body. His gazed moved over her like some kind of laser pointer, with such leisure that she felt swirls of heat everywhere it landed.

A tiny flare of heat in his eyes when it stayed on her tattoos—her half sleeve with a bird flying out of a cage, the one on her lower belly, right above her pubic bone, of a heart, was the only sign that he liked what he saw.

Goose bumps erupted on her skin.

"Turn around," he said, packing a catch and a command, in just those two words.

She wished she didn't like how it pinged over her skin, how it made dampness bloom between her thighs. But God help her, she did. She liked the little lick of heat in his eyes, how his gaze lingered over her tattoos, the way the space around him seemed to crackle with tension. She even liked the taut set of his shoulders as if he was stopping himself from pouncing on her.

Pounce away, she wanted to say, but the words never left her throat.

When she didn't budge, he did a rotating motion with his index finger, his nostrils flaring.

Legs trembling, she turned. When his fingers landed on her hip bones, and he gently tugged her back, she thought she might faint at the dizzy pleasure that claimed her. His warm breath coasted over her back in arousing trails. She could feel his gaze run up every dip and curve of her flesh, up the long, toned length of her legs to her buttocks barely covered in pink panties, lingering on the butterfly tattoo over her lower back and then up toward her shoulder blades where she had a small one of a starling. His scrutiny was thorough and intense enough that her breath shallowed out.

Slowly, she turned back, her own skin feeling two sizes too tight, anticipation inflating her chest.

Another sweep from beneath his lashes and then he gave her a nod. When she met his gaze, whatever desire she'd imagined seemed to have melted away, leaving a cold indifference. "Glad to know you aren't hurt anywhere else."

"What?" she murmured inanely, past the pinprick

of hurt ensnaring all her senses. Then goose bumps rolled all over her bare skin. Her arms shook as she managed to stop herself from wrapping her arms around herself. She was not ashamed, of her body or of the desire she felt for him.

"I needed to make sure you do not have any other bruises," he said, coming to his feet.

"So you made me strip? Under false pretenses?" she said, thanking the universe the tears she felt crawling up her throat didn't coat the words.

"Would you have told me the truth if I asked?"

She opened her mouth and closed it, like a fish gasping for air on land. A draft from some hidden vent in the cabin blew over her skin, making her shiver. Before she could reply, he was in her face again, crowding her with his broad frame, draping the duvet around her shoulders with a gentleness she couldn't abide.

Jia shook it off, merciful anger coming to her aid. "I'm not some…victim you have to rescue."

"No? Because I'm beginning to wonder if your eager proposal wasn't an escape hatch."

"That would only work if I mistook you for a hero, Apollo. But you aren't. So please, don't let it go to your head."

"As long as we're—"

"Far from being a hero, you're a villain, to prey on my family's company, on my family. To use my desire for you to mind-fuck with me is only another step."

His chin tilted down, a flash of anger in his own

eyes. But with a control that was miraculous to watch, he tamped it down. "I didn't mind-fuck you."

"No?"

"I used what I had in hand to achieve what you won't give me. How do you think I've crawled up out the muck your father left us in to where I am today. If that makes me a villain, then yes, I am one."

"Whatever it is that you're imagining about my family, about me, is not true," Jia said, losing her temper.

Fingers on her jaw, Apollo tilted her chin up with such gentleness that tears scratched at her throat. *This is pity*, she chanted in her head but something in his eyes, or her projection of what she wanted it to be… made it so damned hard not to see it as more.

"So your father or brother didn't cause this?"

"No one punched me. I wouldn't have let it go so far."

His fingers tightened infinitesimally, brackets of tension around his mouth. "Did one of them cause this, Jia?" he repeated.

She leaned forward until his exhale stroked her lips, until she could see into the fathomless gray of his eyes and imagine drowning there. Until she could feel the tension emanating from his hard, solid body. And his mouth…a tightness pinched it that had nothing to do with his perpetual grumpiness.

He had played with her, but it hadn't been without cost to him. And Jia needed that equalizer between them more than she needed air. She stepped back and faced him, her body still shaking with anger and unmet need. "You have no rights to my secrets or fears or wants. Whatever little trust was there between us, you've broken it."

He released her. "I see that I've made a mistake."

"What…what do you mean?" she whispered, already missing his feather-like touch.

"Rina *was* the right choice for me."

It was meant to hurt and so automatically, shouldn't, but God, it did. How foolish was she?

She tried to shake it off, used to that kind of casual rejection all her life. When she looked at him though, her belief that he meant to hurt her faltered. He truly believed her sister *was* the better choice. Or that they were interchangeable, except for her talent. And while there were any number of real, valid reasons Rina was a better choice for any man, she wasn't a masochist to try and find out his.

"Of course Rina's the better choice," she said with a scoff.

"As for gaining control of your talent, I could have done it through the board in a year or two anyway. You distracted me," he said, almost to himself.

The admission soothed the little hurt he'd dealt seconds ago. God, the man was giving her whiplash. Or her reaction to him was doing it. "What will you do? Return me with the packaging and the tag intact? Get an exchange deal?"

His mouth curled in distaste.

An uncontrollable shiver went through her again.

"As villainous as I am," he said, magicking a robe out of somewhere, and with firm but gentle movements, pushing her arms through the hole, "I protect my assets at any cost." He tugged the silky flaps closer and tied the sash at her waist, like he was dressing a recalcitrant child.

His gaze found hers and it was like two stars colliding somewhere in the cosmos, leaving an explosion and rubble behind. Only it was in her body. "Especially valuable ones. Even if it's from themselves."

Jia glared at the exit long after Apollo vanished. Shoving her legs roughly into her jeans, she cursed him and herself. She didn't need his damned pity or his honor. And, really, he'd done her a favor by…playing with her desire. He'd shown her that, for him, it was only another form of currency, another weapon.

At least now it wouldn't be hard to resist the damned man.

CHAPTER FOUR

APOLLO STOOD IN his private office and watched as the junior architect team surrounded his wife, peering over her modifications to his initial designs for an eco-resort in one of the Aegean Islands. Her enthusiasm and wit made them swarm to her like bees to honey and it had been so since day one. His staff didn't know he was watching them from within his office and never before had he felt the need to.

He was not a man given to impulses, detours and illogical actions but ever since he'd seen her snoring in his favorite armchair, every rule he'd lived by was suddenly moot.

In the weeks since they'd arrived in Athens, he still hadn't told his family that he and his shiny new bride were here. It wasn't a conscious decision or even the strangest thing he'd done either.

Jia had looked exhausted when they'd arrived at his penthouse in Athens late into the night. Without sparing him a glance, she had moved into the guest bedroom and closed the door.

He wasn't used to having women in his personal

space and while a part of him had been relieved that she wasn't going to encroach on his, a part of him felt increasingly restless with each passing night, knowing she was under the same roof. He wanted her next to him, beneath him, where he could explore all those tattoos day and night.

Now that she'd taken it away, he realized how charming and addicting her easy honesty could be. He hadn't slept well in days now, the fact that he'd hurt her sitting like a weight on his chest.

Which was illogical in itself.

He'd never once cared about how abrupt and aloof he came off to his partners. Work had always been his number one priority and it should be now too. And he was damned if he apologized for something he'd had to do. Better she learn that there were some things he wouldn't tolerate.

To break the ice, he'd brought her into work that first morning, into the offices of his architect firm and introduced her as his latest hire and not his wife. He had a reputation for drawing talent from all over the world.

He'd been eager to see her in action, to see if she was truly as good as she'd painted herself to be. And in the meanwhile, she would thaw and realize that it was ridiculous to freeze him out when he was looking out for her. That he'd give her what she'd so brazenly demanded if only she admitted that he was right.

* * *

Now, three weeks later, Apollo had to concede that she was as stubborn as him, if not worse. Not once in three weeks had she smiled at him or let loose one of her sarcastic comments that put him on edge, or brought up their deal in any way.

If anything, watching her parade in his designer shirts—he'd no idea when she'd filched his stuff— and booty shorts that showcased her long legs and round ass as she cooked breakfast every morning, or those silk slips in the evenings while she played video games in his living room, was slowly driving him out of his mind.

He'd never before cohabitated with a woman, so the experience was unique enough. But wanting a woman's attention and being treated as less than a dust mote was...something else.

Even the shopping spree he'd forced on her on day three by inviting a team of designers with their latest couture collection hadn't thawed her. Usually, it was what he used when his sisters got upset with him. But, instead of enjoying the experience, Jia had simply chosen skinny jeans and lacy tops in different colors, added a couple of work jackets when the stylist commented that her lacy tops might not be suitable for work attire. The whole thing had been done in thirty minutes.

For a woman who wore the same thing over and over, her stuff took over his home. Hairpins, earrings,

bottles of dark nail polish and chocolate wrappers…
he couldn't walk out of his bedroom without seeing
her plastered all across his home.

At work though, she was polite and direct, forever
calling him Mr. Galanis in a saccharine sweet tone
that grated. With everyone else, her smiles, her words,
her actions…were genuine. Enough to turn him into
a grumpy bastard with his staff.

If there had been any doubts about her talent, she'd
ground them into dust. She wasn't just brilliant but innovative, with a fresh outlook toward how living and
working spaces should and would look for a younger
generation. She had not only fit in well with the team,
but in the short time frame of three weeks, she'd made
herself its locus.

Everyone swarmed to her—men and women, old
and young—and Apollo knew she was an asset on
many levels. And yet that word felt cheap and re-
ductive. He wondered what it said that she had sold
herself to him as such and that he had taken her on
as such.

A sudden burst of laughter brought his head up.
One of his brilliant young hires—though Jia was the
youngest—a man named Paulo from Italy, had his
hand on her shoulder and whispered something into
her ear. The more he wanted to go out there and pull
Paulo's hand away from Jia, the more Apollo resisted
the urge. It would only embarrass her and the team.
Christos, he was thirty-nine years old. He should have
a better handle on his baser instincts.

She hadn't even asked him why he'd hidden the fact that they were married. Instead, she'd simply gone along with it and the lack of protest bothered him even more. Was this how Jay had treated her too and she'd simply given in to keep the peace?

The idea of her not fighting him and his dictates made Apollo's stomach knot. As did the idea that she thought he was the same as her father.

Outside his office, Jia smiled at Paulo, replied in English and slipped out from under his hold. When Paulo would have insisted, she flashed her ring at him, a gentle rebuke on her lips. Paulo raised his palms, said something that made her blush and then with what looked like genuine regret, put distance between them.

Having had enough of gawking at her like some lovesick fool, Apollo reached for the door. Even the realization that she had somehow won this battle between them wasn't enough to stop him. He would eventually win the war, he told himself.

Right now, what he wanted more than winning was to kiss his wife until she couldn't ignore him anymore.

Summoned to his office, as if she was nothing more than one of his minions.

He'd never before singled her out during the day. Was he going to get rid of her already? Jia's stomach swooped. Around her, smiles wavered and encouraging comments multiplied. He'd been a demanding, irrational beast for the past week and they didn't even know the half of it.

With each step, Jia felt like a rabbit braving the lion's den. Worse, a foolish, horny rabbit who was ready to beg the lion to consume her whole. Because, damn…living with the man while not claiming wifely rights was like being shown an array of specialty doughnuts but forbidden from tasting.

In the first week, she'd seen it as a reprieve from him, from their arrangement, from her own roller-coaster wants and emotions. Even as an opportunity to prove her worth to him, because that's what this deal was about. Her work was the only reason she was Mrs. Apollo Galanis. His secrecy, while it had surprised her, had also been another reprieve, from his family, the media and the world.

In a way, he'd given her a gift she hadn't wanted or known that she needed.

His Grumpy Assness would no doubt take it away if he knew how much she enjoyed the carefree ano-nymity of being completely herself. *Of being only Jia*, with a chance to prove her mettle, to find a place among her coworkers by her own merit, to be free of patterns and needs that had been cemented over a lifetime. For the first time in her life, she wasn't her father's unwanted daughter, or a resentful brother's sister, or even a protective one, and didn't have to pussyfoot at work or home.

It was only now, away from home and New York, that Jia understood how much her family took up space in her head and her heart. And it was a harsh reminder that Apollo was no different from any of them, except that he was up-front about her value to him.

She'd have even counted the last three weeks as some of the best of her life, if not for the tense evenings and rife mornings with Apollo. Seeing him walk into the kitchen at the crack of dawn, his hair disheveled from sleep, his muscled chest naked, his pajamas hanging low on his hips, made him even more appealing. As if she needed the reminder that the man was sexy in every dimension. If it was power that rolled off him in Armani suits, it was an earthy, easy masculinity that dripped from him in casual clothes.

But she'd found a way to use those awkward, charged encounters to her benefit too. Especially once the thought snuck into her mind that he was hiding her from the world because he was ashamed of her. It wasn't quite a jump since he said he'd made a mistake in choosing her, straight to her face.

Their awareness of each other was bigger than either of them. So she flaunted herself in his oversize dress shirts—even after he'd bought her clothes— took over every inch of his precious penthouse and generally made herself impossible to ignore when he came home.

But she had no idea if any of her ploys to get under his skin had worked.

"Lock the door behind you," he said now as she entered his office, his back to her.

It sounded ominous enough that Jia did so with a mounting heartbeat. But no, he wasn't allowed to see how easy she was for him. Never again. She took a deep breath, and donned her armor before turning around. "Did I pass the test?"

He was leaning against the large mahogany desk, his long legs thrown out in front of him. His office was vast with two different sitting areas, and yet it was dwarfed by him. Tie and jacket gone, his unbuttoned shirt gave her a glimpse of a chest covered in whorls of hair. His hair looked like someone had run their fingers through it, messing it up. He looked like he could belong in a boardroom or a photoshoot, that easy grace radiating off him.

Any hope that he'd reached the end of his tether died when she met his crystalline gray eyes. He looked as inscrutable and unshaken as ever.

"What test?" he said in a voice that rumbled down her spine. It was the first time in three weeks that they were alone together, addressing each other, making eye contact. All the reassurances Jia had tried to tell herself that he wasn't all that irresistible melted away.

"These three weeks at work…you wanted to make sure I wasn't lying."

"I simply wanted to see how you work with a team."

"And?" she said, eager for praise.

"You let everyone's opinions into your head. A little more discernment and a little less people-pleasing would work better for your individual—"

"It's called being a team player," she cut in, ire dancing on her skin.

"Doesn't mean you let all these narrow-minded people dilute your vision. You're brilliant, Jia, and sometimes, you have to be ruthless to give it rein, to meet your full potential."

Whatever protest she'd been about to offer on principle died on her lips. Warmth and a dizzy kind of joy fizzed through her. "That's high praise from the enemy," she said, when she felt his gaze move over her mouth with an intensity that scorched.

"Is that how you still see us?" he asked, straightening.

"Enemies who've made a deal, yes," she said, pressing her palm to her belly, as if she could stop the flutters there. "Believe me, it's better that way."

"You're still angry with me, then?"

What the hell did the man want from her? Why did he care if she was? He'd made it clear that she or her finer feelings didn't matter to him in the big scheme of things.

He simply wanted the truth, Jia, whispered the soft, vulnerable underbelly she always tried to protect.

"Of course not." When he raised a brow, she gave him the truth. At least a part of it. "Let's say I'm not blinded by my attraction to you anymore."

"Because I used it against you?"

"Why ask me when you know all the answers?"

He rubbed a long finger over his thick brow, sudden tension emanating from his broad frame. "I ask because I don't have all the answers. And I don't like not knowing."

"I imagine that would bother the all-knowing Apollo Galanis." Sarcasm dripped from every word. "What is it that you don't get?"

"Why did it hurt you this much? By your own admission, chemistry is not a big deal."

She looked away and then he was there, too close. Her nostrils filled with his cologne and sweat, the air around her suddenly warm with his body heat. His fingers landed on her cheek again. It took everything she had to not lean into the touch, to not give herself over into his hands.

Two fingers became his whole palm. He clasped her jaw and tilted her face up. Warm lights flickered in gray eyes, reminding her of her favorite lighthouse on the bay back home. "Why?"

Something about the way he said the one word got under her skin. She licked her lips, willing her body to stay strong. "Everything else between us is for others. You and my father and Rina and the company and that decades' old revenge, all of it is tainted and twisted. But this attraction between us…it's mine and real and it was the only thing that kept me going."

Her breath became a balloon as she waited for him to push her away, to call her a sentimental fool, to remind her of the terms of their engagement.

Instead, his eyes searched hers, as if he wanted to

plumb the very depths of her. His large hand spanned her jaw until the pad of his thumb rested against the pulse at her neck. She could feel its thrashing beat against his flesh, begging for something she shouldn't want.

"I should very much like to kiss you, Tornado. Now."

"To seal the deal now that you know I'm actually good? To keep me compliant enough so that I'll give it my all? To give me just enough to keep me panting—"

His lips fused with hers, and a shuddering breath left her, leaving trails of agony in its wake.

"Because you're right, and this is too good and too real to not celebrate," he whispered against her mouth and there was no turning back.

Jia rubbed her lips against his, and his hands wandered from her neck to her shoulders to her hips. He pulled her flush against him, her arms went around his shoulders, her fingers sank into his hair and he was kissing her as if he meant to devour her whole.

It was different, this kiss, rough and heavy with three weeks of desperate wanting.

He was different, and it showed in how he licked and nipped at her lips, how he demanded access and swept his tongue through her mouth, how he lifted her until she wrapped her legs around his waist as if it was a move they'd performed for years.

His unfiltered need stoked hers. His mouth at her neck, trailing down to the valley between her breasts, made her breath shallow out. Jia writhed herself against his growing shaft, her mouth dry, her head dizzy with pleasure. He was hard and thick and she wanted more.

Pressing her back into the wall, Apollo rocked his erection into the cradle of her thighs, hitting the exact spot where she needed it. How she needed it. Her eyes nearly rolled back in her head at the pressure building, roiling. God, she might come just dry humping him like this and she didn't even care and...

Suddenly, the door to his private office flew open and four women of varying ages stood in the entryway, eyes wide in their faces.

"*Apollo!* Shame on you," said the oldest woman, and Jia wanted to sob because her release was flying away and her lower belly felt empty and abandoned and she thought she might never get the one thing she'd given herself permission to want from her husband.

Apollo released her legs from around his hips with a muttered curse, and still holding her, straightened her top and jacket with gentle care. Jia hid her face in his chest. His quick buss at her temple and harshly whispered reassurances made warmth curl through her. And she wondered, in that lust-heavy haze, if protecting her wasn't simply protecting his asset but something more.

Just a sliver more.

Just a teensy bit particularly-about-her more.

Her knees trembled when her feet hit the floor, but he held on, and Jia had the craziest thought that he would always catch her, no matter what. And the thought was both exciting and terrifying.

"Apollo! Explain this! At once!" the older woman repeated in fractured English.

Jia snuck a quick look at him and was bemused to see a strip of dark color streak his cheeks.

She turned but remained behind him, reluctant to meet people who'd hate her on sight, just when she was getting used to him. There was no doubt who these women were.

"Hello, Mama. Hello, Christina, Chiara, Camilla."

When it became clear that Apollo wasn't going to budge from his place—he couldn't even if he wanted to for Jia was clinging to him like a jellyfish—his mother advanced into the room while one of his sisters closed the door.

"You arrive in Athens three weeks ago and don't even tell your family. You don't bring your new bride to meet us. And when I come into your office to give you a piece of my mind, I find you kissing some teenage…"

"Floozy," one of the sisters supplied helpfully.

Apollo's mother shook her head, and Jia's respect for the women grew, along with the hysterical chuckle in her chest.

"Kissing a work colleague, while already neglecting your bride?"

Jia giggled. Loudly and disgracefully, and even

muffled into Apollo's muscled back, it sounded alarmingly flippant.

"The floozy dares to laugh at us, Mama," the one who seemed to be the oldest sister supplied in flawless English, looking truly angry. "This is what your son has reduced us to, our family to, in his pursuit of revenge, and what he has turned—"

"You were always one for drama, Camilla." Apollo finally spoke. He didn't desert Jia though. No, he pulled her from behind him, and wrapped an arm around her waist. "Mama, *this is* my wife, Jia. Jia, this is Mama and my sisters—all older than me. The one who held judgment is the middle one, Christina. The one giggling at us both is Chiara and the one spewing fury is the oldest, Camilla."

For long, awkward moments, Jia could do nothing but stare at them. They were all tall, with distinct, almost overpowering features, all cut in the same mold as their brother. And yet, where they all missed the mark of true beauty, something had come together just a little differently in his case, and the result was a stunning, gorgeous man.

Her man, if she let herself believe him.

"Very nice to meet you all," she said, "though I wish it was under different circumstances. That's why the inappropriate giggling."

His mother sighed while Camilla didn't look one bit mollified.

Jia tried not to crumple under her refreshed glare, which meant she was remembering who she was.

"Hello, Jia," his mother said. Kindness shone from her eyes as she moved forward, her gaze eating her up as intensely as Apollo's did. "I'm sorry for barging in and yelling at you. I didn't realize Apollo's wife was—"

"Barely older than a teenager," the one called Chiara supplied, mischief in her eyes. "All these years, Mama, we keep pushing mature, sophisticated women toward him and turns out Apollo has a taste for young—"

"I admit he's of a different generation than me," Jia rushed in, wanting to shake them as much as they were doing to her world, "but your brother's like...a stud and I've always been into that whole age-gap, smoldering alpha-hole thing, so it works."

Mouths fell open and hit their chests. Again.

Jia bit her lip, regrets flooding in. God, she'd always gone on offense when she felt cornered.

Chiara and Christina burst out laughing while Camilla's glare intensified. His mother's eyes twinkled. With pleasant surprise, Jia hoped.

"You are different from what we expected," she finally said.

"She's full of surprises," Apollo said, his eyes full of that wicked humor and a sliver of something that sounded like pride. No one had ever shown that emotion on her behalf. Jia felt like grabbing his face and kissing him all over again. Audience be damned.

"Why didn't you tell the staff that she's your wife?" Camilla said, clearly still spoiling for a fight.

Whether her ire was directed at her brother or Jia, she had no idea. But Jia didn't want the whole story about how their marriage was nothing but a deal to be exposed in front of these women. Clearly, they cared about Apollo and didn't understand his actions after all these years, any more than she did.

It wasn't that she wanted a good start with Apollo's family, not when she was going to leave, sooner or later. But she couldn't take more taunting, on top of everything her own family had doled out at the mere idea of this relationship. And that kiss, before they had been rudely interrupted, was as real as anything Jia had ever known in her life. Or more, even. She didn't want it tainted by everything else that surrounded it.

"That was my idea," she said, riding the impulsive train all the way. "I wanted to start work and bond with Apollo's team without any preferential treatment. Also, there's the fact that your brother's too much of a workaholic to take me on a honeymoon. This way, our first few weeks of marriage are both secretive and spicy. And just for ourselves."

They stared at her, as if she were an exhibit Apollo had checked out of a museum. It wasn't just that she was the enemy's daughter, but how she dressed and her tattoos and everything about her, Jia realized. She didn't doubt she was as different as possible from Apollo's previous…interests. The mere thought of them made her stomach knot.

"That kiss we interrupted was definitely something," Chiara added.

Jia blushed. Their mother shushed her.

"So you work here, Jia? And you plan to continue working with my brother?" It was the middle sister, Christina, this time. There was genuine curiosity in her question.

"I'm an architect, and, yeah, I plan to continue working with Apollo. It's one of the reasons he was so…moved to steal me for himself. On top of our crazy chemistry, I mean. We understand each other even in our work."

The words left her of their own accord and Jia realized the truth of them only then.

For all their age gap and enemy vibes, Apollo and she shared the same kind of vision for their work, for how they wanted to shape the world around them. For how they changed it.

Flushing, she turned to look at Apollo, who was frowning. As if she was putting out main character energy when she should be in the back with chorus.

She pinched his side, which was all rock-hard musculature and didn't really give into pinching, and then winked at Christina. "To be honest, I'm trying to make sure he doesn't forget what a delight I'm to be around twenty-four hours, seven days a week."

Christina stared at her brother and Jia for long moments. After a while, she extended her hands to Jia. "Welcome to the family, Jia. I have a feeling you're exactly what my brother needs."

She kissed Jia's cheeks even as her statement rang hollowly through Jia's gut. If she let herself, she would see romantic crap in everything. Just as she was forever searching for the slightest hint of approval in her father's words and gestures.

Apollo's mother and other sisters followed suit, air-kissing Jia's cheeks. Talk moved slowly to their non-wedding in New York, the hurry for it, and inevitably to Jia's family and how Apollo was taking over the family company.

On that front, Jia couldn't summon even a fake smile. Around her, English morphed into Greek and determined to wait them out, she stood there, like a statue frozen amidst life.

But when her father's name came up and a flash of such intense hurt crossed Apollo's mother's face, all the armor Jia had cloaked herself in fell away. The sisters watched as the son and mother argued in rapid Greek and then joined in. Only Christina seemed to be arguing on his side. Finally, his mouth set into that arrogant tilt that no one could budge, Apollo stepped away.

Oh, why had he insisted on marrying one of the Shetty daughters knowing it would hurt his mother to even have the shadow of Jia's father touch her family? What did he hope to accomplish except fill them with doubts about her and himself? Would having control over her fate go such a long way toward appeasing his thirst for revenge? Why had Jia thought this would be as simple as bearing undeserved judgment and anger from his family?

Pain was something she was familiar with and it danced in his mother's eyes.

Impulsively, Jia reached out and took the older woman's hands. "I'm sorry that my very presence causes you such…anguish. For what it's worth, I apologize for all the pain my father caused your family. It was inexcusable and if I could change it, I would."

Stunned silence met her foolish declaration. Even the fiery Camilla, it seemed, had nothing to counter it with.

Jia tried hard not to look at Apollo. She couldn't bear it if he thought her statement was pandering to them or if he mocked and dismissed the sentiment itself.

Apollo's mother shook her head, one rogue tear running down her cheek. "Children are not responsible for their father's sins. Or their failures," she bit out.

Out of the periphery of her vision, Jia saw Apollo flinch.

The older woman gently clasped Jia's cheek and a soft exhale left her. "Christina was always the smartest of my children." The other three protested loudly. She laughed, wiped her cheek and, leaning toward Jia, whispered, "You're exactly what Apollo needs. Let's hope he doesn't realize it or he will…" She sighed.

Leaving Jia to wonder what she meant by it and why it felt so unbelievably good to be welcomed by his family when they should hate her on sight.

When they finally left—nothing short of Apollo's promises that they would be at the family home that very night had achieved it—Jia made to follow them.

Hand at her elbow, Apollo stopped her.

Pressing her forehead to the cool door, Jia refused to turn. She was feeling emotional, and the last thing she wanted was to betray something he'd consider ammunition in this battle of theirs. God, who'd have thought being married to the enemy would be this hard on her heart?

For a man who didn't deal in feelings, Apollo seemed to understand her reluctance to face him. His arms came around her waist gently and pulled her until she was plastered to him, chest to thigh. It wasn't a sexual embrace but neither did it feel like a transactional kindness. It was something in between, like their relationship itself, teetering between labels.

"I didn't marry you to punish you."

"No? Because from where I stand—"

She didn't finish her statement because his mouth was at her neck. He nibbled at her fluttering pulse and Jia melted into his arms, her muscles instantly loosening and tightening of their own accord.

"You were right. Whatever this started as, there's this very real thing between us, *ne*?"

"Is there?" she asked, arching her neck to give him better access. Dampness bloomed between her legs when he gently nipped the spot.

"Yes, Jia. Maybe I should have said this that very night you begged me to marry you and—"

Jia knocked her elbow into his gut and grinned at his surprised grunt.

"Or maybe at our wedding," he said, turning her to face him. His gaze held hers, something shimmering in it.

"Said what to me?" she said, hanging at the edge of a rope, desperately aching for something.

"I see you, Jia, and everything you are. And a little more that you hide."

Gratitude and something more joined the arousal in her limbs, making her dizzy.

Bending, Apollo pressed a kiss to the corner of her mouth, his large hand cupping her hip, as if he already knew all the nooks and corners of her body. "So, let's celebrate this with a real wedding night. Whenever you're ready."

His promise reverberated through her as Jia went back to her open cubicle and tried not to hear the frenzied whispers around her. For the next couple of hours that she lingered at work, no one would meet her eyes, or respond to her without looking at her as if she'd suddenly turned into a bug-eyed monster. Paulo, when she forced him to respond, couldn't get away from her fast enough.

The reprieve was over. His family knew, her co-workers knew and now, the whole world would know that she was Jia Galanis. And yet, as she repeated to herself a thousand times, and relived the moment when Apollo had looked into her eyes and admitted that he saw her, Jia didn't feel trepidation at all. If anything, she felt excited about this new, temporary relationship more than she ever had about a real one.

CHAPTER FIVE

APOLLO HADN'T MEANT to leave her to the curious, even aggressive in Camilla's case, clutches of his family. He had just decided to bring her home, right before they had descended on them en masse.

But after, even though he'd taunted her that he wanted his wedding night, he'd sent her to his family home with his chauffeur, claiming a work emergency. Long past midnight, he had returned to his penthouse.

Whatever he thought he was escaping by sending Jia away, duplicitously no less, smacked him in the face when he walked in. From the vast sitting lounge where she'd spread around her sketching papers to the kitchen where she'd abandoned spice tins and tea boxes and chocolate hampers, to the large media room where her video game equipment lay scattered about, she had already stamped the space with her presence.

The silence without her was different from the one with her, and he realized how companionable even that had become between them. As if they were an old couple, married for fifty or so years, easy with each other in everything, like his grandparents were. Even the bathroom—week two she'd begun using the one attached to his bedroom, claiming a woman needed the more luxurious one—didn't remain untouched. There was a box of tampons on the black granite.

He'd found her sobbing one evening, hair in a messy updo, pillows clutched to her chest while watching some old Bollywood flick. When he'd demanded to know what had upset her so, she'd stuffed more chocolate into her mouth and bit out that she always cried like that on her period and would he please leave her alone. He had sat by her, pretending to be absorbed in the colorful movie that he didn't even understand, and then fascinated when she started explaining the convoluted plot, forgetting her usual frosty silence.

None of his sisters had ever complained or sobbed or made such a mess of themselves on their periods, he'd thought. But then, when had he had time for any of them, either growing up or after their father had died. For all he claimed to do for his family, he'd had very little to do with his own for the past two decades. Something Mama hadn't missed pointing out in the three minutes they had talked to each other.

Several hairbrushes, a bottle of perfume and tubes of lipstick surrounded his sink, mocking him. He almost lifted the bottle of perfume to sniff it like some lovesick fool when he caught his reflection and stopped.

Walking back into the kitchen, he poured himself a glass of wine and then discarded it. Even the damned wine reminded him of her. Remembering Jia got headaches from red wine, he'd already asked his housekeeper to stock more whites.

Then as he moved through his bedroom shedding his clothes and donning sweats, the source of his restlessness finally hit him.

I'm sorry for everything my father did to your family, she'd said.

No one could doubt her apology had been heartfelt, not Camilla. Not him. And yet, her words and her expression haunted him, holding up a mirror into which he didn't want to look.

He'd thought telling her that his marrying her wasn't meant as a punishment would be enough. But was that true of his intentions, or the impact it had caused on her life? Knowing her now, knowing how he'd uprooted her from her family, without even her familiar things, knowing he'd thrust her into the center of his family, knowing how prejudiced they would be against her, what was it if not punishment?

For close to two decades, he'd worked himself to the bone, neglecting his relationship with his mother and sisters, neglecting his own happiness and comfort, pursuing wealth and connection and power, with one goal in mind.

To ruin Jay Shetty's company and his peace as he'd ruined theirs. To push him toward despair as he'd done to Apollo's father. And along the way, he'd deemed it okay to include the old man's family. He'd known Rina didn't wanted to marry him but he hadn't cared much about it because all it took was for her to naysay her own father, right?

Not his problem.

But now, when he remembered the ache in Jia's face when they had all argued about her family as if she wasn't standing right there, her easy, blunt honesty and her apology as she faced up to what her father had done when she'd been no more than a child, her flirty answers so that the coldness of their deal wasn't exposed to his family... Apollo wondered at the sanity of what he had done. Wondered suddenly about all the possibilities of a future that he had stolen from Jia.

Did she have a boyfriend back home? A lover who was even now mourning her loss? What were her dreams, other than rescuing her useless family? Why didn't she work for some other company instead of letting her brother pass off her work as his own? Why the desperate effort to save a family who seemed undeserving at best and loathsome at worst?

He knew nothing of her hopes and fears. But more importantly, with the little he did know, Apollo didn't want to give her up.

She was Jay Shetty's daughter, she owned the stock that Apollo needed, and she was one of the most innovative young architects he'd ever met, and keeping her as his wife would be a lifelong, painful thorn in the old man's side. Especially since he would make sure that Jia shifted her allegiance completely toward him.

Anything less than complete surrender was unacceptable to him in his wife, on principle. But even more, from the woman he was fast becoming obsessed with.

All the fun, parties, peace and comfort, and even sex, that he'd given up in his twenties and most of his thirties, he would make up with her. The prospect of spoiling Jia and himself, of glutting himself on her, with her, breathed new life into his burned-out soul.

As he pushed his muscles beyond endurance on the rowing machine in the state-of-the-art gym—one place Jia hadn't invaded because she claimed she was allergic to sweat—he shifted his view of this marriage he'd insisted on.

Whatever he had taken away from Jia, he was sure, was small and pathetic enough that he could replace it. He'd drown her in wealth and recognition and laurels for her work, lavish her with gifts and luxury, so much so that all that fierce loyalty she showed her undeserving family would soon be his.

He would have all of her, and he would make her happier than Jay ever had and *that* would be the best revenge.

Two days later, it was midafternoon when Apollo stepped out of the chopper he'd called in at the last minute. Usually, he enjoyed the two-hour-long drive from his headquarters in Athens to the eco-friendly mansion he had built for his family nearly eight years ago.

It was one of his favorite projects, a contemporary but warm design set on fifteen acres of land—a gift to his mother. Although she'd never been as happy or receptive about the gift as he'd expected her, even needed her, to be. Neither did he forget that she wouldn't have even moved in if not for Camilla, who, after a nasty divorce that had left her with nothing, had wanted her boys to have a good life.

Christina, whose partner, Fatima, was a world-renowned artist and traveled quite a bit like him, had been the least challenging about accepting gifts from the wealth he had amassed. Among all of them, she was the outdoorsy one, and the idea of living on fifteen acres of land, surrounded by her family, held great appeal for her. Being the compassionate one, she was also the one who had tried to understand what had driven Apollo for so long, though she never quite supported him either.

Chiara, whose husband had failed at several businesses, had three children, and Apollo was more than happy to support her and her family.

And yet, he hadn't visited the estate more than twice, and not once in the last two years.

As he walked the gravel path heading up to the mansion, he felt a strange elation in his gut, as if his return this time was more significant than it had ever been before. Was it because he had finally reached his goal of defeating the man who had ruined his family's happiness? Or was it simply a need to see the woman who had occupied his thoughts for the last two days?

Whatever it was, Apollo decided he would accept the feeling, as another gift after his long struggle.

As soon as he crossed the threshold and walked into the large living area with its high ceilings and exposed beams, he heard her laughter—deep, husky and without reservation. Pleasure drenched him, a fist of need tightening his gut.

Sunlight streamed through the high windows, dappling the light furniture and dark hand-stained wood floors in beautiful contrasts. The scent of delicious food emanated from the open kitchen, where he could see his mother, Christina and Chiara fighting and shouting and slaving over the stove. Chiara's husband was chopping vegetables.

Apollo had to take a small detour to see past the pillars into the cozy great room. Up on the opposite wall, the huge plasma screen TV showed off some role-playing game in high-definition color. And standing behind the coffee table with controllers in hand were Jia and Camilla's sons on either side of her, whooping and squealing and shouting as they killed some many-pronged creature on the screen.

A short distance from them, caught between the kitchen and the living room, was Camilla, watching the trio with naked envy on her face. Apollo remembered his mom telling him that Camilla was having a hard time connecting with her sons, who were now sixteen, and were starting to ask more and more questions about their papa.

As if aware of Camilla's gaze on her back, Jia

turned and beckoned his older sister, holding out the controller. One of Camilla's sons joked about his mother not knowing anything except handling a spatula in the kitchen. Jia paused the game and told him off with no hesitation.

Only then did Apollo allow himself to look at her properly.

His wife, it seemed, had an allergy to clothes and, *Christos*, he was determined to fix it. Cutoff denim shorts that covered her ass, thank the saints, but showed off her long, toned legs. Paired with a teeny-tiny crop top that left inches of flesh between the hem and the shorts, she looked like she could be an older girlfriend that one of his nephews was forever trying to show off.

Under the anime T-shirt, which Apollo realized belonged to his nephew, her colorful tattoos peeked out. Her hair was in a messy bun again. Stubborn strands kept falling into her face, which she pushed away with the back of her hand. Sunlight picked out the golden highlights in her hair, just as it shone on her skin.

She looked good enough to eat, and he was ravenous for a bite.

He walked into the lounge and landed a soft slap over his nephew's shoulder. The monster thingy that Jia had almost killed on-screen ate her little elf avatar in one quick gobble, while she watched horrified, unmoving.

His other nephew groaned and burst into broken

English about how they'd almost had him and why had Auntie Jia suddenly lost focus.

Grinning, Apollo leaned his head over her still, tense shoulder and grabbed the controller from her. She jerked as if his touch scalded her. He threw the controller to his nephew who caught it with nimble fingers. Then Apollo grabbed her hand and tugged her behind him.

She stumbled once as they passed the enormous kitchen and his mother and sisters called out greetings to him. He waved at them, barely adjusting his stride.

When they reached the open, hanging stairs past the corridor, Jia seemed to come to herself and dug in her feet. "What happened? Where are we going?"

"Which one is our bedroom?" he said, going down one step so that he could look at her. The steps were made of wood and hung unsupported on one side, opening out into the other living room, while the glass walls on the opposite side gave magnificent views of the wild gardens outside.

Industrial-size pendant lights cast a soft glow as evening slowly gave way to pitch-black night.

"The big one with the attached suite on the second floor," Jia added almost automatically. "Your mother said they saved it for you and your wife."

"Perfect. Come."

"Why?" she said, watching him with wide eyes. Her mouth was soft and pink and reminded Apollo of how much he liked sweet and tart strawberries.

"There's something I would like to show you."

Doubt shone across her face. "In the bedroom?"

"Ne."

"And it can't wait?"

"Ohi."

"Well, I'm not in the mood to see anything. You send me here with them, ignore me for two days and then show up here, demanding I...pay attention to you? *No!* I was in the middle of a game and then Maria was going to show me how to cook this dessert I love, and Christina and I planned to watch a horror flick, and Chiara said she'd do my nails. I'm not pushing all that off because Your Arrogant Highness has decided he wants to show me something."

"Fine," he said, leaning closer. *Christos*, just the scent of her was enough to twist him into a mass of need. The red rose undertone to whatever she used...it had begun to linger on his clothes, around the sheets and towels, and damn if he hadn't begun to chase it all across his penthouse like a junkie. "I'll simply order them to not do any of those things with you until you attend to me."

"Attend to you? You're not my bloody—"

"I have a wedding gift for you."

Her eyes widened and her lovely mouth fell open. She was all lean, taut curves but her mouth...it was wide and lush and utterly sensuous. And he loved how she melted when he licked it, how she jerked when he nipped it. "You do?"

"Yes."

"And that's what you want to show me?"

"Among other things."

She blushed then and it was the most glorious sight Apollo had ever seen. Her gaze slipped to the small gift bag in his hands and then back to his eyes, via a lingering detour at his mouth. Her soft exhale coasted over his lips, taunting.

The little frown was back between her feathery brows and he swallowed an impatient curse. Only now did he understand what a distrustful creature she was. Just like him. "Why can't you show it to me in front of everyone?"

"I didn't want to embarrass you. But if you prefer—"

"No, they're already teasing me because I made up all that stuff in your office," she said, stepping down and then walking up with him.

He hid his grin. "*Why did* you make up all that stuff? Why hide the reality of what this is?"

"Your mother and sisters…" A soft, almost wondrous note entered her voice. "I could tell at one glance how lovely and kind they are. How much they adore you. My family already thinks I've betrayed them. There was no point in letting yours see what a monster you are."

"I thought I was a villain, not a monster."

"Interesting that you see the distinction."

He laughed and like clockwork, her gaze clung to his mouth.

"Tell me."

A breathy sigh. "A monster can't help acting on his instincts."

"Ahh… I'm growing in your estimation."

She shrugged, just as they reached the landing and then started up the second set of stairs. "This home… Maria told me you designed and built it. For her."

It was his turn to shrug.

"I spent the first day just exploring all the clever little nooks and crannies. Every inch of it gets natural light. And, oh, my God, that office on the ground floor… You used the wood from the trees that were cleared to make space for the home, didn't you?"

He nodded. "We used every inch of it that we took from the land."

Not even a sunbeam could match the brilliance of her smile. "It's the most beautiful home I've ever seen, Apollo. Like, if I was given a choice where to live the rest of my life, it would be here."

He was stunned enough to stare at her. This time, the pleasure that filled him was…different, almost insidious in nature, creeping and settling into places and pockets he hadn't realized were empty in him.

"What?" she demanded as he continued to stare at her. "No one can deny you're a brilliant artist. Although, you haven't done anything like this in the last few years, right?"

"Something like this?" he said, awed at this woman who so easily saw through to his burnout that no one, not even Christina, had seen.

"This place is kind of magical. Your latest designs are much more…commercial and soulless."

"Ouch," he said, laying a hand on his chest.

"Tell me about how the solar panels work. All the glass must make it cool in winter but I saw that there's no central heating."

It was the last thing Apollo had expected her to ask him. No one in his family had realized how special this project was to him. Which was why Mama's almost instant rejection and continued refusal had hurt so much. "My father was the one who did the initial designs," he said, finding his voice suddenly rusty.

Jia smiled, running her hands over the dark wood banister. "I thought it had an old-world charm to it. You know, I've looked at some of his plans for the eco-cabins they were designing back then. I found them in the archive's office..." She slowed down when he didn't respond. "My mother used to talk about him sometimes. I was curious enough that I went to the archives."

Shock suffused him enough that he simply stared. When a regretful look came into her eyes, he hurried on. "I didn't realize they were still there."

"She hadn't been exaggerating. Your father was... had a very unique touch."

He gave her a nod, unable to speak past the sudden lump in his throat.

"So this home...you modified the initial plan?"

Apollo told her, at length, as they walked up the second set of stairs. With each word he said, and each step they took toward their suite, and each memory he unlocked, some hard, petrified thing in his chest cracked wide-open. And he found himself breathing deep and long, as if he'd been only half-alive until now.

It was easy, and a strange kind of wonderful, to talk to Apollo about the design of the house.

Jia had never fallen in love faster or deeper in her entire life. It was as if the house was a physical culmination of all the dreams she hadn't even allowed herself to feel.

The high ceilings, the exposed wood beams and pillars, the open expansiveness of the plan…even the hand-stained hardwood floors and the lighting fixtures, every inch of it spoke of the attention and love he'd poured into the house. More than anything else, it spoke of the man and the beat of his heart.

Which had then made her feel foolish because Apollo Galanis had no heart and what was more proof than the fact that he'd not only kept her identity secret for three weeks among his staff, but then dumped her with his family, while he did God knows what for two days.

And now here he was, demanding attention, dangling a gift in front of her face just when she was determined to hate him all over again. Or better, become indifferent to him.

She walked into the vast bedroom suite, which had glass for ceiling and three walls, enchanted by it all over again when she realized he'd fallen silent behind her.

"You like the house, then?" he said so softly that for a second Jia wondered if she was imagining the sliver of vulnerability in it. But his eyes remained hard and inscrutable. There she was again, projecting her own feelings into his words.

"I do," she said, wanting desperately to find that sliver again when she shouldn't. "Is there a reason you haven't let anyone photograph it?"

Leaning against the closed door, he shrugged.

Jia didn't miss that he did that when he didn't want to answer a particular question.

When he lifted the small bag in his hand, excitement beat a thousand wings in her belly. The unnerving intensity of his gaze as it swept over her, up and down, sent a shiver through her. "Is it a guilt gift or pity gift?" she said, brazening it out.

He cocked a brow, arrogance dripping from the very gesture.

"Guilt because you did something you shouldn't have in the last two days. Pity because you ignored me and feel sorry for me."

He threw his head back and laughed with such abandon that she felt helpless against the sensuality of it. A river of longing ripped through her. She stared at the corded column of his throat, the deep grooves around his mouth, the way his thick, rigidly cut curly hair flopped onto his forehead.

He looked…heart-meltingly gorgeous and he was hers, that foolish voice whispered. When his laughter died down, it still colored his eyes, making them warm and deep.

"Well, which is it?"

"I want no one but you, Jia. I'm committed to this marriage."

"So pity, then," she said, some unknown thing fluttering in her chest at the resolve in his eyes. "Not needed because, honestly, I like your family. I'd even say the appeal of this marriage increased tenfold when I count them all in the package."

He placed his palm on his chest, mock-flinching. "You don't like being ignored."

"I don't like that you control everything in this relationship."

"And yet, I wasn't the one who executed the Three-Week Frost," he quipped with a mock shiver.

"You made up a name for it?" she said, laughing despite her intention to stay strong.

"It was the coldest I've ever been in my life."

And now, she was the one melting…

He pushed off from the door with a deliberate grace that sent her heart thundering in her chest. It was ridiculous to flee because she wasn't scared of him but she took a step back. Eyes now a molten gray, he stalked her across the vast room. When her bare feet touched the cold wood past the rug under the bed, he took a detour to turn the fireplace on. Another thing she'd noted—how he took care of the smallest thing that caused her discomfort, how he was always watching out for her.

Then he was there, caging her against the dark wood bookshelves, which lined the only wall that wasn't glass. "Jia Galanis…scared of a little gift?"

She squared her shoulders and tilted her chin. "I'm not scared of you or anything you do."

"Then open it."

She took the bag, made a face at him when he laughed at her trembling hands. Her heart decided to take on Olympic speed as she pulled out a dark blue velvet box. She wasn't a huge jewelry person but this was a gift. And she could count on one hand the number of gifts she'd received in her life. Most were before her mom had died when she'd been thirteen.

Slowly, she undid the latch on the box and there, nestled in a soft, velvety cushion was a thin, exquisitely made gold necklace with tiny, detailed leaves and a teardrop sapphire in the midst. It was exactly like the one piece of jewelry she'd coveted all her life but wasn't allowed to have.

Tears filled her eyes and a strange urgency beat at her. The necklace almost got twisted in her trembling fingers before Apollo steadied them. When he lifted it, to put it around her neck, Jia jerked away. "I want to put it back in the box before I…break it."

"Jia—"

"Put it back, Apollo," she said, nearly yelling.

"Okay," he said in a tender voice that threatened to break her apart. Then, as she watched like a vulture circling prey, he nestled it back into the box and closed the clutch.

Jia grabbed the box from him with a proprietorial jerk, opened her little backpack and shoved it inside. When she straightened, he was at her back, crowding her with his broad, lean frame. His arms came around her waist, his large palms resting on her belly, and without her meaning to, without her permission, her body relaxed into his hold.

She allowed herself the luxury of his tender embrace for a few moments. "Where did you…how…"

"I asked Rina about your interests. She's feeling guilty enough that she stole into your father's locker and photographed it for me. I commissioned the piece. I was waiting to pick it up before I flew here."

She looked up sideways and his gaze caught her as easily as if she was a floundering fish. "Why?"

"I wanted to give you something that you would like. Giving you something that you'd never been allowed to touch was better. I didn't expect to make you cry," he added in a droll voice that didn't quite mask his concern.

Jia hesitated, reluctant to answer the hidden question. But he'd taken a step toward making this more than a cold, business arrangement, hadn't he? This gift and those words in his office…as much as it terrified her, she knew it was time she took a step too. At least, in her own head and heart. "That piece was my mom's. My father gave it to her. She wore it for special occasions only. She's…" her voice broke just at those two words "…she's the closest thing to my heart."

"Tell me about her."

She shook her head.

"Jia…"

"No. Some things are too precious to taint as ammunition between us."

He stiffened around her, his disappointment as visceral as the thundering beat of her heart. "Your wants and your fears and your dreams," he said, repeating the words she'd thrown at him on the flight. "You guard them as if they were a treasure."

But Jia didn't relent. Couldn't. "They are foolish and simple. Of no value to you."

"This was a horrible gift, then," he said with a scoff, releasing her.

Jia turned and fisted her fingers in his shirt, refusing to let him go. "No, it isn't. It's…the best gift anyone's given me. Especially since I know my father will never let me have the original." When he looked doubtful, she hid her face in his chest and breathed him in. He was solid and hard and warm, his heart thundering under her cheek. And now, she wanted to take a thousand more steps toward him. "I don't want to fight with you. Not after you gave me such a…special gift."

CHAPTER SIX

JIA THOUGHT HE'D push her away and the very prospect sent dismay curling through her. He'd called Rina, made the effort to find out what would please her, and then he'd had it commissioned, blasting through all the fake, false armor she'd draped herself in. It was more than anyone had ever done for her.

Maybe she was giving him too much credit for a little gift—she was that deprived of basic affection—but she couldn't help it.

After what felt like an eternity of her clinging to him, his fingers came into her hair. He roughly yanked the clip she'd used to put it up and his fingers circled her nape and then crawled up to tilt her face up to him. "I will have all of your secrets, Jia. Willingly, from you."

It was a promise and something more, but she didn't have the will to challenge him anymore. "You won't take what I more than willingly, wantonly offer," she whispered, and then on a dare, she went on her toes and dug her teeth into his chin. It was a possessive gesture but she didn't care. This was the most freedom and selfishness she'd allowed herself in her life and she wanted to drown in it. *In him.*

A gasp escaped her when he lifted her and deposited her on the desk.

"You're right. I'm a poor husband, *agapi*," he said, tugging at the hem of her blouse until he could pull it off her head. A sudden blast of cold air hit her skin.

Shock and arousal flooded her system, releasing a riot of shivers through her. His big hands cupped her shoulders, palms rough and abrasive, his body heat a sliding rasp against her front and his mouth… his hot, soft mouth was at her lips. Nibbling away the last of her defenses.

Jia's groan seemed to emerge from the depths of her being.

Apollo kissed her roughly, nipping and biting, barely letting her breathe while his hands drifted down from her shoulders to her back. Her strapless bra came loose and her nipples puckered.

Shivers overtook her, of a different kind this time, when he cupped her small breasts and the pads of his thumbs flicked at her nipples. Jia arched her spine, each little flick arrowing down straight to her core. When he pushed her with a hand on her shoulder, she bowed back as if she was made of nothing but elastic desire.

Steely eyes held hers as his tongue laved at one nipple and then the other, before he drew it into his mouth with rhythmic pulls. She jerked at the stinging pressure, slowly lapping over into shivering waves all through her. When she tried to rub her thighs, his thigh blocked the movement. She made a keening sound in her throat, her arousal winding and tugging concentric circles in her lower belly. Eager to do the same to him, she scooted forward on the desk.

She undid the buttons on his shirt roughly, until she could reach warm, taut skin. Holding his gaze, Jia stroked her palms all over him—the hard planes of his chest, the rough down of his chest hair and the ridged muscles of his stomach. With each stroke of her hands, the gray of his eyes deepened.

When her hand drifted to his crotch, he captured it, lifted her hand, and pressed his mouth to her wrist. Both hands arrested, Jia leaned forward and rubbed her bare breasts against his chest.

He groaned. The rough brush of his chest hair against her sensitive nipples was both torment and pleasure. His attention on the slide of their flesh, he released her hand. Jia snuck it down his abdomen until she could cradle his erection. With a rough grunt and a rougher curse, he rocked into her touch before he caught himself.

"You're cheating," he said, his hands caressing her breasts with such thoroughness that she forgot what she meant to do.

"All's fair in lust and war," she said, craning her body into his touch.

Grinning, he paid her back in full. As if he had all the time and energy in the world, he started all over again, trailing kisses down her jaw, between her breasts and down to her belly button and then back up.

He teased and tormented her nipples with his tongue, sucked them into his mouth, grazed them with his teeth until Jia was writhing on the desk, a mindless wanton made of nothing but nerve endings, spiraling and fragmenting. Her climax was a taunting mirage just out of reach. When his hand went to the seam of her shorts, she stilled.

He licked the shell of her ear, his voice a husky taunt. "If you're not ready for more, it's fine. But let me make up for ignoring you for two days."

She looked up, honey pooling in her veins. "They're all out there and can probably hear us. I couldn't face them if—"

"What do you think my sisters do with their partners?"

She blushed. "I…it's the middle of the day and—"

"All you have to say is 'not now,' *pethi mou*," he said with a tenderness that threatened to break her into pieces.

"No. I want this. I came prepared for this."

"That sounds like an exhausted, put-upon wife bracing herself for her marital duties."

She looked up and the humor in his eyes undid the sudden tension that seemed to have overtaken her. "No, I mean I was… I was looking forward to this. I started the pill before we left."

"But?" he said.

Jia thought he'd meant to say something else but

changed tack at the last second. "No buts and ifs. I want this, Apollo. You have to give me a little control though."

His smile was wicked as he moved his hands in a *have at me* gesture. But the tension in his body was unmistakable. Suddenly, it didn't feel like she was the only one drowning. And Jia realized that that was the root of the problem.

His gift, horrible as he called it, had shifted the current between them and she felt as if she'd been splayed open for his benefit. Knowing he was as gone for this heat between them…made her feel better. Made her feel equal and wanted, at least on this surface level.

Pressing her mouth to the warm, hard skin of his chest, she busied her hands with the zipper on his trousers. His black boxers went next. Impatience coating her skin with a tremble, she barely pushed them past his hips when his cock popped out.

A fresh set of flutters began between her thighs. Wetness soaked her thong when she fisted his length and gave it a tug. His head thrown back, his chest heaving, Apollo looked like one of those stone sculptures she'd once seen at the MOMA. But warmer and harder and so…more achingly real than any perfect marble bust could be.

Jia increased the speed of her fist, acting purely on instinct and feeding on his reactions. She traced the slit in the head with the pad of her thumb and when it came away wet, she sucked the pad into her mouth.

Apollo let out a filthy curse. "Jia…you drive me wild."

"You taste…" Jia swallowed at the dark cavern of want opening up in his eyes "…like decadence and arrogance and all the filthy desires I never admitted to myself."

Fingers circling her nape, Apollo pulled her in for a near-brutal kiss.

Whatever little freedom he gave her, it seemed, was over after her outrageous little comment. A sudden puff of cold air against her folds told her he'd ripped her thong off. And then his fingers were there, coasting and stroking over her inner lips, draping her wetness all over. As she watched, her breath a shallow whistle in her throat, he brought his fingers, coated with her arousal, up and then painted it over her nipple. It was filthy and freeing and set Jia on a spiral she didn't want to stop climbing.

And then his mouth was on her nipple, sucking and licking, tasting her arousal and groaning, even as his fingers went back to her folds to resume their torture.

Assaulted from all directions by sensations, Jia felt like she was riding a crashing boat on rough waves in the middle of a storm. He was everywhere, his lips and fingers driving her out of her skin, setting a mad pace she couldn't follow, until he speared her with a broad finger and hit a particular spot deep inside her.

Jia jerked against him, her thighs a vise around his hand as her orgasm crashed through her, thrashing her this way and that. A sob escaped her throat, along with her panting breaths.

Apollo didn't relent.

His lips tugged at her painfully sensitive nipple and he kept the base of his palm against her clit as wave after wave settled into tiny jerks and languorous aftershocks. Fingers in his hair, Jia clung to him, clung to the clove and pine scent of his warm skin.

Her flesh cooled, but she wanted more. She wanted all of it. This was all she was allowed of any relationship in a long while and, God, this was all she was allowed to ask and want and own of *him* and she wasn't going to settle for anything less than claiming all he would give.

Even as her spine trembled and her thighs felt like she'd run a marathon, she straightened and caught his mouth in a kiss. While she hadn't allowed anyone to come close after her first and only disastrous relationship, she'd allowed herself kissing. And now she used every inch of her experience to tangle her tongue with his, to sweep it through this mouth, to bite and nip at his lower lip until she could feel his tension mounting. His touches became harder, deeper, his caresses wilder and rougher, leaving little divots in her willing flesh.

She ran her mouth down his jaw to his chest, peppering kisses and bites all over his taut skin. It was warm and salty and suddenly, she wanted to taste him somewhere else. She wanted his cock in her mouth, and him a little out of control. No, a lot.

She wanted him to lose it all.

His grip in her hair tightened when she wrapped

her fingers around his cock and gave it rough, hard strokes. "Let me down," she whispered, skating her mouth down to his tight abdomen.

"Not today," he answered roughly, and then he was shoving her hand away, pulling her closer and rubbing the head of his erection all over her folds. The sight of him against her was erotic and intimate.

Jia braced herself on his hard muscles, her entire pulse centered there where he played with her.

"You're ready for me, *agapi*?"

"God, yes, Apollo," she repeated and before she could catch her breath, he entered her with one smooth thrust.

Jia jerked and stilled, like a fish caught on a bait. It pinched a bit. No, a lot, bordering on hurt. It had been so long and even then, it hadn't been all the way like this.

Slowly, the delicious soreness faded, breath by breath. Nothing in the world could equal being tethered to Apollo like this. She had a feeling of being utterly full and tight, and when she wiggled her ass on the desk, he shifted inside her and the pinch faded and a spark of pleasure sputtered through her.

Then it went out.

Chasing it, she thrust her hips and tested the fit again, and heard Apollo's rough grunt. And then she didn't have to do anything, because he pulled out almost all the way and stroked back in. Not as deep as the first stroke but teasing and taunting her with it. Trying what would drive them both to the edge.

And slowly, in tune with his thrusts, her own climb began all over again and they found a rhythm. Jia raked her fingernails down his chest, nipped at his flesh, clung to him like a rag doll as his thrusts gained momentum.

The desk banged against the wall and she, apparently, was quite vocal when it came to pleasure and Apollo's grunts were not quiet. When another short but powerful orgasm began to rip her into so many pleasure-filled fragments, she told him how good it felt, how much she liked it when he pinned her with his hips, and then, sweat dripping down his forehead and holding her gaze, Apollo mouthed a filthy word and shuddered when his own climax followed.

It was very late that night when, finally, Apollo was free to do as he pleased.

As Jia had predicted, they had been interrupted that afternoon, minutes after they had *finished* with loud bangs on the door to their suite. They hadn't even separated yet.

In his urgency to get Jia alone, he hadn't let his mother or his sisters tell him that they had invited around hundred guests to celebrate his and Jia's sudden union. A wedding reception, Mama had said with a glint in her eye, so that their extended family, long-standing friends and his grandparents could meet her wonderful, new daughter-in-law and bless this very real marriage.

He had been in such a hurry that he hadn't even

noticed the staff putting up marquees and tables outside. The reason why they had all been so busy cooking, even with outside catering ordered.

While Apollo had fixed his clothes and responded to Chiara banging on their door with a catlike grin, Jia had disappeared into the bathroom and locked herself in. He hadn't seen her again until the evening when she descended the stairs behind a beaming Chiara.

Apparently, his wife had made a deal with Mama—in exchange for donning a dress and deserting her usual lacy tops and short shorts tonight, Mama would teach Jia how to cook.

To say he was stunned, by her negotiations with his mother *and* her look, would be an understatement. It was becoming clear that not only had she won them over in just a few days but his mother and sisters had already gained her trust. As if she was blossoming in a different way under their honest and yet tender care.

Still, as only Jia could, she retained her own style, and that little fact pleased him way out of proportion. For all the rigid requirements he'd held on to in his head for a wife for years, he wanted to change only one thing about the one he had now.

In a shimmery copper satin dress with flimsy straps and simple bodice that rippled like dark water when she came down the steps, Jia had looked soft and pretty as if she'd been tamed for one evening. And he liked that. Liked knowing that her true wildness was all his.

Only his.

Against the shimmery satin of her gown, her skin glowed and her tattoos stood out. The one at her collarbone, a bird in midflight, looked like it was fluttering its wings with how fast her pulse beat at her neck. Her hair pulled back and put up, called attention to the fine bones of her face, drawing out the fragility she hid beneath her tough attitude. Was that what her sisters and mother had already seen?

And had he, the arrogant fool, once thought her anything less than stunningly beautiful?

When she was almost to the bottom of the stairs, he noted the necklace nestled at her throat. The leaves and the pendant shone brilliantly against her skin, almost blending into the tattoo on the other side.

Catching his gaze on her neck, she smiled. A tremulous, hopeful one that he'd never before seen on her lips. He had never felt such feral satisfaction as he did at that moment, at seeing her sweet joy, knowing that his gift pleased her. Not his first million, not when he'd won multiple awards, not even when his goal of nearly two decades had finally been within reach.

The boisterous arrival of his extended family had saved him from examining the feeling too closely.

And now, as he walked up the stairs to his suite, he wondered at how that feeling still persisted, at how smoothly and irrevocably Jia seemed to fit into every aspect of his life.

He found her in the large claw-foot bathtub, in relative darkness except for a few beams of moonlight and a couple of flickering candles. The ceiling was all glass, which meant one could sit in the bathtub and view the stars. It was one of his favorite features in the house.

Candlelight and moonlight seemed to battle to bathe her silky skin in an ethereal glow.

As he closed the door behind him and leaned against it, her eyes opened. Shadows danced there and he wondered if the evening had exhausted her. His family could be a lot.

No, withdrawn, he amended, on second thought.

Why, he thought with a fierce protectiveness he had never known before. If someone had said unkind words to her because of who she was, they would face his wrath.

He had always wanted to provide for and protect his family, especially after Papa's death, but this was different. This feeling had its claws deep in his bones. Was it simply his new determination that he would own everything about her?

"Hey," she said, clutching her trembling lower lip between her teeth.

Pushing off from the door, he started unbuttoning his shirt. "Can I join you? Or would you like to play the tired-tonight-honey wife card?" he added, desperate to make her laugh.

She smiled and it just touched her eyes, pushing back the earlier shadows. "I thought that was when you wanted to avoid sex."

A lick of fire came awake in his veins as her hazy

gaze swept over his bare chest and lingered over his fingers at the band of his trousers. He unzipped and kicked off those and his boxers. Her mouth fell into an O, on the wave of a soft, helpless gasp.

As if tuned into that husky pitch of her, his cock grew to stiff attention.

"So you're not averse to it," he said, grinning. Pleasure was a river dragging him along in its undercurrent and he didn't want to let up, not even for a breath.

"Not when you give it so good."

He laughed, desire and a strange kind of joy fizzing through his veins.

"Plus, I have been given loads of advice, from your grandmother to your aunts as to how to manage you."

"That sounds ominous," he said, sliding into the tub.

It took a moment for her legs to settle between his, her feet ending up on his thighs. He grabbed one and kneaded the high arch.

She let out a hiss of pleasure, head thrown back. Water droplets clung to her long neck, inviting his mouth to lick up. "Christ, Apollo, is there anything you aren't good at?"

She sounded so put-upon that he grinned. "Was anyone unkind to you? My aunts and cousins can be blunt and voluble."

"No, if anything, they were all extra kind and open. Like I said, giving me all kinds of tidbits as to how to manage you." She punctuated that by drawing on his chest with her foot. "Apparently, I have saved you from a horrible, loveless existence."

When he tracked his fingers up her ankle, she pulled back with a giggle.

"Then why the shadows in those beautiful eyes, *matia mou*?"

"What?" she said, startled enough that she slid a little lower in the tub.

Apollo used the chance to pull her to him. A little stiff, she came into his arms reluctantly as if she didn't dare trust him, even after the afternoon they'd shared. It annoyed him that she always held something of herself back. It was the very trust he wanted, was beginning to crave even in waking moments.

He would figure her out, he promised himself.

He settled her legs around his hips and she relaxed, her core pressed right over his shaft, and they groaned. He stole a soft kiss, liking her like this, all wet and soft and malleable. But he wasn't about to let himself get distracted.

"If no one was rude to you, why the sadness?"

She shrugged and hid her face in his neck. Her armor was showing holes, he realized, with that weird pride slash satisfaction.

"Jia?"

"I just…" Tears swam in her eyes when she looked up. She wiped them with the back of her hands and scoffed, the sound full of self-deprecation.

"Tell me, *parakalo*." Even that word, which he barely said to anyone, came easy with her.

A shuddering wet exhale shook her slender shoulders. "Your family is…like my dream family. They fight and argue and yell at each other, but beneath it all, there's this thread of acceptance and love."

She whispered the last as if the word might reach out and bite her. Then she cut her gaze away and he knew it was because she didn't want him to see it. "I couldn't help…wishing mine was remotely like that."

"My family is yours, Jia."

Her gaze was stricken when it met his, as if the very idea was impossible.

"You can let the old one go and embrace this one. Especially since they all adore you already."

"Spoken like a ruthless billionaire," she retorted but there was no bite to it.

When he grabbed her hips and rubbed her folds against his erection, she groaned. The hiss of pain beneath that sound poked a hole through his haze of lust.

"You're sore," he said, arresting her hips when she'd have repeated his actions.

"It's been a while," she murmured, her tongue lapping at his shoulder like a cat.

"How long a while?" he said, her mouth playing havoc with his control.

She looked up, and frowned. "Am I allowed to ask the same question?"

"About…three years. Don't even remember her name," he replied. "I've been busy—"

"With taking over my father's company," she said,

nodding. Then she scrunched her brow. "Seven years and once, technically but not quite."

She never said "our company," he noted with a spark of anger on her behalf. "So I didn't pull you away from a young, ardent boyfriend?"

She rubbed her cheek against his and moaned when his stubble scraped. "It's a little late for that question."

He gripped her chin in his fingers, stopping her exploration. Willing her to meet his gaze. "Not an answer."

"Why all these questions now?"

"I'm curious."

"I've only ever had one boyfriend if you could call him that. I was eighteen, and we met in secret because my father wouldn't have approved. He was a musician."

"Ahh...the tattoos," Apollo said, his voice dry. That this old, far-gone lover had left such a mark on her made him intensely jealous.

Jia grinned and scraped her teeth against his chin, before peppering soft, warm kisses against his jaw-line as if she was mapping the contours of his face to memory. "Jax did encourage me to get that first tattoo. But the rest are all mine. A kind of rebellion, if you really want to know. My father hates them."

And yet, she sought his approval in other ways. Didn't she see that? "So what happened?"

"It never took off to last." Then she pulled back and searched his eyes. "You really want to know?"

"Yes," he said, grabbing her by the tight indent of

her waist. "The sooner you tell me, the sooner I will give you what you want."

"That's sexual blackmail," she said, grinning. Then she sobered. "Jax…was a decade older than me. He wanted to travel the world. Travel and music were his passions and he wanted me to leave with him."

"That's quite an ultimatum to issue to an eighteen-year-old," Apollo said, immensely glad she hadn't left with him. But it also meant that her martyr-like need to save her family had not only been present then too, but it had alienated a man who might have cared for her.

Apollo didn't understand it; she was so smart, worldly and tough in every aspect of life. But with her leeching family, it was like she willingly put on blinders.

"He…changed his plans for me. Even got a job to show me that he could do boring nine-to-five. He waited for me to be ready for a lot of things. But when we actually started seeing each other regularly, all we did was fight. He thought I should move out, stop coddling Rina, stop…" A sigh rattled through her. "He thought my family was a shackle and that he was nothing but entertainment on the side for me. That last time it blew up, we were in the middle of it, literally. He stopped, dressed and left. Never looked back."

"Do you regret it?" Apollo asked. "Not leaving with him?"

This time, Jia hid her face in his throat again. "It's

pointless to look back. And he should have known better than to ask me to choose him over them."

"Is that a warning, Jia?"

"You're a clever man, Apollo Galanis. You figure it out."

It provoked him to no end. Before, Apollo didn't want them to have her loyalty, because he wanted to be the victor in this little game. Because he wanted everything she had to give for himself.

But now he wanted her to see for herself how blind and undeserving her devotion was. How she had limited herself all these years, for them. That it was that very trait that had brought her to him…threw him into confusion.

He lifted her gently and slid his fingers to her center. *Dios mio*, she was wet and ready for him. "Should I remind you that you have thrown your lot in with me?" he said, finding her clit and flicking at the bundle.

She jerked and arched against him, the plump points of her nipples sliding deliciously against his chest.

"Do you need a reminder that your stock in the company in three years, your talent, your work, *you* are all mine?" he said, pumping one and then two fingers inside her.

Mouth lax, eyelashes fluttering, she threw her head back and let out a moan. His cock became painfully hard as her muscles squeezed tight around his fingers deep inside her.

"Or maybe you want to argue a little more about this and I should stop?"

She stilled and then in a violet fury of movement that splashed the water around them, cupped his cheek and took his mouth in a filthy, possessive kiss that said everything he had without using words. "All I want," she said, nibbling at his lips, "for myself is this—" something fierce and feral glowed in her eyes "—and if you deny me this, Apollo, if you take this away from me..."

"I won't," he vowed, cherishing how freely and easily she gave of herself here. How from the first moment, she had honestly and bravely faced this attraction. It was the most arousing thing about her—that fierce attitude and that honest, scorching desire for him. For now, it was enough. That she wanted this with that fiery need was enough. The rest he would have soon.

"Come for me, Tornado," he said, pinching her clit between his fingers.

She wrapped her fingers around his cock and squeezed, licking the shell of his ear.

"For tonight," she said, nipping at his earlobe, "can we come like this? Together? Tomorrow, I'll be less sore—"

"This is all I've been thinking of all day, *agapi*. You falling apart for me. You not hiding anything from me."

And then they were kissing again, and their hands were everywhere, their bodies weaving together and retreating in the water, and Apollo thought he'd never been more eager and desperate, never tasted such bliss before.

Already familiar with his body and his want, she stroked him harder and faster. He gritted his teeth, fighting the oncoming wave. He wanted, needed, to push her over first.

She was writhing and twisting around his fingers, but her eyes, so wide and clear and penetrating, never left his. As if that was the thing that would send her to the edge she was seeking.

"This is going to get messy," she said, arching into his touch, and the stubborn thing that she was, she never let her own strokes falter.

Apollo grinned and laved at her lower lip. "I had a feeling about that when I found you snoring in my armchair."

She laughed then, and that's how they came together and came apart and Apollo wondered at how addictive this woman could become.

If she hadn't already.

CHAPTER SEVEN

SHE LOOKED LIKE a wraith, sweaty and feverish, amidst a cloud of navy-blue bedsheets. Stilling at the entrance to their bedroom, Apollo tried to work through the turmoil that had gripped him ever since she'd fallen sick.

In a mere two weeks since she'd fainted at work midday, Jia had already lost weight.

It didn't matter that the team of doctors he'd summoned had reassured him that it was a very bad case of chest infection. Or that his mother and sisters took turns tending to her and feeding her when Apollo had to leave her side. Which, to be honest, hadn't been much.

He wasn't the best person to nurse someone in such fragile health but the thought of deserting her when she was weak and vulnerable didn't even merit consideration. At least, Mama had convinced him to let the nurse he'd hired check on Jia every few hours, in case he missed any turn for the worse.

For the first time in his adult life, he was behind on deadlines for two different projects, his two assistants were constantly reminding him about the things he was pushing back, and one billionaire client, and an old friend, had jokingly threatened to cancel when Apollo had told him that he had no bandwidth to look at his design modifications. Apollo's reaction to that had been telling on many levels.

It felt like a personal affront to Apollo that she would fall this sick under his care. He and his entire family were all healthy as oxen so where had Jia caught this illness? Had he driven her too hard by having her work long hours with his team so soon after taking her away from her family? Had he demanded too much of her at work and in bed? Had she been unhappy? Shouldn't he have seen the signs that she was unwell long before she'd fainted at work?

When he sat by her, he felt restless, useless…and worse, helpless. Which he'd never been good at abiding. Still, a strange, horrible fear that she would slip away if he left had kept him glued to her side, night and day.

He didn't require a degree in psychology to understand that it reminded him of the time that Papa had started taking to bed at all hours of the day.

He had been crushed by Jay's deceit, devastated by having to sell most of their assets to pay off overdue bank loans. Had hated the fact that they'd all had to move back in with their grandparents. Nothing they'd done had stirred him from the fugue.

Mama had urged Apollo to concentrate on his own studies, that whatever Papa was going through was a temporary thing. The small malaise had lasted for months. Until one day, Apollo had found him lying still on his bed, his face pale and all his vitality gone, overdosed on painkillers.

And he, Apollo, had done nothing to help him. Which had set him on a path he hadn't budged from in two decades.

"Why do you look so angry?" The whisper-thin question from the bed jerked Apollo into the present.

Sweaty hair sticking to her forehead, Jia looked small and pale, as if the infection was doing its best to dim her. Except her eyes, which finally had that sparkle back. She raised her arm, smelled herself and then fell back against the sheets with a sigh. "You can come closer. I don't stink."

Despite the volatile mix of emotions churning through his gut, his mouth twitched. This was the spirit he had missed in two weeks, the Jia he was coming to see as the prize for all his struggle. The only prize worth winning and having and keeping.

Only a month and a half of marriage, and she had embedded herself under his skin, and he wasn't even sure if he wanted to pull her out. He'd blindly and arrogantly stumbled onto the best thing in his life and for a man who reached his goals on his own merit and strategy, it was unsettling as hell. Because what was the guarantee that it wouldn't be snatched away from him? Especially, since he'd done nothing to deserve her.

"Who do I have to thank for the latest sponge bath? I smell like my favorite red roses."

Without answering her, he pressed the back of his hand to her forehead. She was damp and sticky. "I think your fever's finally broken." His hand shook as he reached for the water glass, so great was his relief. In its wake, exhaustion hit him like a full body assault. Grabbing a straw, he dunked it into the water and pulled her up a little so she could drink it.

Her eyes stayed on his face as she sipped. *Dios mio*, how he had missed that playful, challenging, sometimes downright angry gaze on his skin…and sometimes so addictively open in its wanting.

Unable to help himself, he tucked a thick lock of damp strands behind her ear. He wiped a drop of water from the corner of her mouth, feeling his heart finally settle into a normal pace.

"You didn't answer my question."

"Which one?" he said, settling near her legs.

With a rough exhale, she pushed off the sheets, and looked down. The cotton top stuck to her skin and her shorts had ridden up all the way. Sitting up, she adjusted her clothes. "Who gave me the last sponge bath?"

He wrapped his fingers around her ankle, his gaze caught on a small red heart tattoo there. "How did I miss this one?" he muttered to himself.

"You're way too focused on my breasts. And another spot further south."

When he looked up, she was grinning. It sparked

a chain reaction in his chest, some feelings known and acceptable, and some…downright debilitating.

"You owe me two answers," she said, her gaze sweeping over his face intently.

"I was the one who gave you all the sponge baths. You were docile as a lamb, for the most part. Though I can tell you I prefer you as you usually are."

"Mistrustful and argumentative?" she said with a self-deprecating laugh.

"Rearing to take me on," he added, running his thumb over the tattoo.

"Wait." Color flushed her sharp cheeks and it was a welcome sight. "You were present…when I couldn't walk to the bathroom, and the other day when I threw up…"

"All me."

She buried her face in her hands, groaning. Then she lowered her fingers. "And when I had that really bad dream and woke up thrashing?"

"I got into bed with you." And he had stayed with her for the rest of the night.

"You were here the entire time? The whole time," she said, her chest rising and falling as if she'd reached some impossible conclusion.

He felt insulted that she found it shocking he would look after her. What did she think he meant by *commitment*? And what did it mean that he couldn't make himself leave her side?

"Your fever was too high and you were delirious. The doctor said someone should be with you every minute. Plus, you've got your fingers stuck in half the firm's projects, so there wasn't really a point in me harassing the rest of the team for progress."

Pushing her hair away from her face, she sighed. "So you're angry that everything's backed up at work? That was quite the ferocious expression you had earlier."

It was the perfect out for Apollo to take. But then, he'd never harbored self-delusion. "I was frustrated. And I'm not the greatest at sitting patiently doing nothing."

"That's quite shocking to know," she said, sarcasm dripping from each word. "Why frustrated though?"

"No one can tell me, apparently, why you got so sick."

Her mouth slackened. And then she smiled. And Apollo felt as if his entire world had turned upside down. "Apollo, there can be a hundred reasons why I got sick. And—"

"Yes, but the rest of us are well. Only you got sick. I don't like it. Nor was the speed at which you've been recovering to my liking."

"Oh, I'm sorry that I'm not recovering fast enough to please Your Grumpy Highness." And then, because she was Jia, she tossed a throw pillow at him. It hit him in the chest and dropped to the floor.

"Now I know you're truly on the mend," he said, getting up and walking toward the door. She'd need more than the broth she'd been surviving on to recover. Suddenly, as if a switch had been flipped, his entire workload slammed into his brain, claiming his attention.

"Wait, Apollo."

He turned to find her combing her fingers through her hair and pulling it into a knot. The action pushed her breasts upward, her nipples poking through the silk top. Her stomach looked even leaner than before. The desire to hold her gripped him like a vise but it wasn't just the base lust to claim, own and find that delicious edge. It was more.

Whatever she saw in his gaze, a flush climbed up her chest and neck. Like a newborn calf testing its legs, she got off the bed gingerly.

Apollo went to her just as she stumbled and she fell against him with a huff. And then her hands went around his waist, and she clung to him. "Thank you for taking care of me. Even if I cost you thousands."

"Millions, Tornado," he said, his voice strange to his own ears.

She dragged her teeth against his chest roughly, teasing and provoking him. And he realized a great big thing that he'd overlooked all this time. Willingly enough, she'd given him everything she'd had ever since walking into his penthouse.

Except now, he wanted the thing she thought she didn't have.

He held her loosely, sudden itching to get away from her. From himself in this state. But she was soft and warm and sweaty in his arms and he had missed her lithe body, her tart comments and how hard she made it to gain an inch of her trust but when she did…

"I take my vows seriously, Jia," he said, pressed a kiss to the top of her head and then walked out.

Jia stood under the double-jet shower after Apollo left and tried to make sense out of her knotted thoughts. Before they turned into feelings and wishes and hopes and foolish dreams.

But she was afraid that she was already too late.

The fact that Apollo hadn't left her to herself; the energy and hours he'd put into looking after her…she didn't know what to make of it.

He was a billionaire…he could have given her care over to any number of staff. Even his frustration that she wasn't getting better fast enough…had cloaked something far deeper. She was sure of that, even as she warned herself not to make it into a big deal.

Her mind spun in circles as she stepped out of the shower and looked at herself in the mirror. She'd lost weight just in two weeks and looked even more angular than usual. But her eyes, even sunken, held a glow, as if a small flicker of joy had been lit up within. Work life where she was noticed and respected, a family that offered unconditional acceptance and care, and a man who respected her and challenged her and then turned her inside out with his demands at night…

Wiping the steam from the mirror, Jia let herself speak and see the truth. For all that she'd been sick, she was happy within. A kernel of hope had taken root in her heart and it was already changing her. And she knew she could get addicted to the illusion of this happiness with Apollo. That if she wasn't careful, she'd fall into the trap of wanting more and more.

She needed to stay strong, like she had during her mother's illness even as she had realized finally why she fit differently into her own family. All her life, Mama had loved her, but the cost had been being good, being quiet, being the best daughter and sister Jia could be because Mama hadn't wanted her father to find fault with Jia. She had let it dictate every action and numbed the whispers of her heart.

Her arms shook as she pulled on sweatpants and she tried the warning in her head again. Like everyone else in her life, Apollo's approval and affection for her came with a cost. And yet, neither her heart nor her body believed it one bit.

A few days later, Apollo was finishing breakfast when Jia came down the stairs, her phone pressed to her cheek. It was cowardly but once he had known that she was on the mend, he'd fled to Athens and stayed at his penthouse. He'd dropped by this morning with the convenient lie that he needed her to look over some designs.

Now, her eyes blazed with anger when they met his, and her throat moved on a swallow.

Irritation flared through Apollo and it took all the willpower he possessed to not grab the phone from

Jia and smash it into so many bits. He had no doubt who the caller was for he had dealt with the matter only last night. His wife's spineless sister, Rina.

The very idea that he had almost married her made bile rise through him. If not for Jia's fierce loyalty and courage, his life, right now, would have been very different. The realization grated on him.

"You…insensitive, lying bastard!" Jia said, running down the last two steps, fury dancing on her face.

Apollo shot to his feet and caught her as she tripped on a video game console and almost took to the floor. *Christos*, she felt breakable in his hands, all crackling fury and no substance beneath. Around him, his mother and sisters came to attention.

"Jia—"

"You promised you'd leave it alone, Apollo," she was yelling now, pushing at his chest with her fists. "It's the wish you granted me. But even that's not sacred to you. To think I was actually beginning to believe you and trust you—"

"Stop it, Jia." Apollo grabbed her hands before she could beat at his chest again. Tears filled her eyes. Alarm rang through him, making his words sharp. "You're going to make yourself sick. You've barely recovered and—"

A bitter laugh escaped her mouth as she roughly wiped her cheeks with the back of her hand. "Oh, please, don't pretend as if you care."

"Jia, listen to me—"

"Apollo! What did you do?" his mother said, joining in.

Apollo gritted his teeth and prayed for patience he didn't have. The last person he wanted to discuss Jia's family with was his mother. She'd never understood his drive for reparation, *his madness for revenge* as she called it. He definitely didn't want her to know the particulars of his and Jia's marriage or all the ways in which her family used her.

It might have started as a business deal but their relationship had already morphed into something else, which he'd been struggling to make peace with. Damned if he was going to let his family see their marriage differently, see him differently, just when he was beginning to see the error of his ways.

"This is between Jia and me," he said, hoping they would take the hint.

When none of them budged, he met his mother's gaze. She looked miserable, as if Jia's pain was her own. All his sisters, even Camilla and his rowdy nephews, glared at him, ready to take him on if Jia only gave them the word. "Please," he said, addressing Mama, "trust me."

And this too felt like a rite of fire because he could see Mama struggle. Had he fallen so far in her estimation that she assumed he would hurt his wife on purpose?

Finally, she nodded and herded the rest of them out of the living room. He wrapped his arms around Jia and thanked the saints he didn't believe in that she didn't push him away.

"You promised you'd leave it alone," she repeated, subdued and stiff. "Instead, you had cops haul Vik away. You're ruining my family and I've lost the last chance with my father to…" She sighed.

So that's what had sent her into such a…temper? Had her father somehow pinned Apollo's actions on Jia? How did he think she would control a powerful man like him?

His chest felt tight, a painful kind of powerlessness clutching him in its hold. With every fiber of his being, he wanted to get rid of this hold her father seemed to have on her but he couldn't. He hadn't been able to stop the damage done to his father and it felt like he was in the same boat again.

This time, the obstacle was an invisible, intangible thing and if he pushed the matter, he would hurt the only innocent in all this.

"Your blasted brother nearly took your eye out. You shouldn't be protecting him."

"He just lost his temper," Jia said, pulling back. "He was…drunk and upset that I married you without telling them. We got into an argument and he was stumbling and pushed me. I fell against the edge of a table. That's the truth."

"He's a twenty-eight-year-old man," Apollo bit out. Just the image of her brother pushing her was enough to send him into a rage. "He should have better control of his temper."

"Maybe yes, but he doesn't deserve to go to jail for it and—"

"Did Rina tell you he pushed her too last week?"

"What?" Jia said, blinking hard. "She was crying and my father was yelling in the background—"

"He pushed her. They had to bring her to the hospital—"

"Is she hurt?"

"No, she insisted on going because apparently she's pregnant and wanted to make sure everything was okay."

"She told you all this?"

"Last night, between sobs," he said, dryly.

"She's…pregnant?"

"Yes. Which is why she shamelessly pushed you toward me. What little courage she might have, she used it up telling me she'd have just married me anyway *if* you hadn't interfered, and it felt awful that she'd let you take her place and, oh, please would I help her because your father was going to throw her out, and she found out from you that I wasn't the horrible monster she thought I was."

Jia rubbed her hands over her face, a ghastly calm taking place of the frenzy from before. "Vik…he adores her. He shouldn't—"

"Why is it okay for him to push you around but not your older sister who's supposed to look after you?"

"That's ridiculous," Jia replied and turned away, but not before he missed her flinch. All her fury was spent and he could see her withdrawing into herself, as clearly as if she was setting up brick walls around her.

"No, Jia," he said, grabbing her around the waist until she looked at him. "You started this, *agapi*, and I demand that you finish it. You and I both know Vik needs to learn a lesson, before he does something worse than getting drunk and pushing his sisters around. If your father had any kind of sense, he would let him rot in the cell and fear the consequences."

"Fine. I agree."

"Then please, kindly answer my question," he said, unable to keep his temper out of his tone.

"It's a ridiculous assumption."

"Jia—"

"How does it matter who looks after whom? You're the youngest but you take care of all of them, don't you?"

"My sisters don't take advantage of me. Mama hates everything I have done for the last decade but she would never sell me out to some stranger who might or might not—"

"My mom asked me to look after them, okay?" Jia burst out, her eyes flashing. "To keep them together. All my life, she begged me to be good and quiet and capable and strong…stronger than any of them. She said it was her fault that my father had become so hardened and soulless and she couldn't desert him and I shouldn't either."

"What weakness?"

Something like pure anguish danced in her eyes. It stole the breath from his lungs.

"She...she had an affair and I was the result. When she found out she was pregnant with me, she confessed everything. My father...loved her enough that he agreed to raise me as his own."

"So Rina would've followed in her footsteps if you hadn't saved her?"

She glared at him but didn't argue. Apollo wondered if that was progress. "I didn't...know until I was thirteen, when Mom fell sick. I finally understood why he was so...strict and unbending, especially with me. I promised her that I would be strong, that I would take on her responsibilities in her absence."

Suddenly, Apollo had a blueprint to every little thing that had thrown him about her from day one. The emerging picture only served to anger him. "So you'll forgive them anything? Forgive your father because he raised you as his own, even though, clearly, he expects you to pay for it?"

"He's never asked me for anything." She pushed her fingers through her hair, her gaze far off for a moment. "I... I did it willingly. And not everything is black-and-white, Apollo. Would you forgive me if I cheated on you?"

The very idea made him want to howl like a deranged person. "I'm not answering that because I know you won't." He had no idea where his faith came from. But it was there, unwavering and real, as solid as the house they were standing in. Stronger than any conviction he'd ever had before.

"The fact is he loved her enough to raise me as his. He gave me a home, an education, a family."

"But he continues to punish you for it."

"He's never said one unkind word to me my entire life."

"He pawned off your work as your brother's—"

"Because Vik was about to lose his job. We agreed that it would be a one-time thing. Even the black eye," she said softly. "He didn't know that Vik pushed me. I never told him that Vik loses his temper when he gets drunk. You can't blame him for something he's not aware of."

"Ahh...you have such little expectations of the people around you, *matia mou*. By that measure, our marriage should hopefully last a hundred years."

"At least he met my expectations, little as they were," she said, tilting her chin. "Unlike you."

Her silken thrust found a raw spot, one he wasn't aware existed. To be compared to that man with no morals and to come away wanting...felt like the worst kind of defeat.

But then, he was discovering a lot of things hadn't existed for him before this woman. And yes, some were to be expected because he had never been married before. But he was also aware of doubts where there was only certainty before and of a hundred little changes in his thoughts, in his actions.

He raised a brow, refusing to let her see his dilemma. Needing for her to come to him, to ask him for what she wanted. She unbalanced him so easily, that he was always looking for leverage in their relationship. He hated losing in the slightest, and the stakes were only increasing.

"You gave me three wishes. You broke the third one."

"What would you have of me, *pethi mou*?"

A flicker of warmth shone in her eyes before she rubbed her eyes with her fingers. The action reminded him of how painfully young she was. "Will you help Rina out please? For me?"

He sighed, even as he felt a contracting tightness in his chest. As if his heart was too big or his body too small to contain these...feelings she evoked. He couldn't explain it or banish it. Because he had tried to, when she lay in bed, all of her fierce vitality doused.

"I have," he said, loathe to make her beg when it came to her damned family. "Her lover has a job with the New York branch."

"Already?"

"You keep forgetting that I know you now, Jia. Maybe better than anyone else."

Something soft and vulnerable sparked in her eyes before she chased it away.

"Your third condition is for you to use," he said, knowing he was playing a very dangerous game. But then, he was a man who had taken big risks for the things he wanted. It was how he'd made a name for himself and millions for his family, how he'd risen to the top and become powerful enough to take on the man who had ruined his father. And this...this game he was playing with his wife and her as the prize, it was the biggest battle of his life. "*For you, Jia.* Not for anyone else."

"Good to know," she said, digging her teeth into her lower lip. She scooted closer, her fingers fisting his shirt in a possessive gesture that made his blood pound. "Although, anything I want from you for myself, I have a feeling you'll give it freely."

"Such faith," he said, gathering her to him. She was even more slender than before and yet, somehow, if he closed his eyes, he knew he would only see her gap-toothed smile, and her vibrant attitude and the soft vulnerability she rarely showed. But he was getting little slivers of it now. "You have to do something for me in return."

"What?"

"Get back to bed."

"I've just spent two and a half weeks there. And this recovery period is worse. I'm lonely—" faint color dusted her cheeks "—and I have all this sudden energy."

She looked so sparkly and cheerful that Apollo didn't have the heart to point out that it was because he had agreed to help her lying, cheating coward of a sister. If she let them, her family would suck the marrow out of her. "I'll ask Christina to join you and keep you company."

"No."

"Camilla, then."

"God, no. She'll make me drink that awful bone broth again."

"You need it."

"I know what I need."

"What?"

"You, in bed, with me." When he only watched her without replying, she pouted. "I mean, I adore your family, yes, but I want you."

His mouth twitched, despite his resolve not to give in. But he was angry and disgruntled enough with her, disturbed enough by her revelation about her mother and her father that he wanted to be persuaded. Seduced. Wanted. He'd never before in his goddamned life wanted to be wanted.

"Please, Apollo. You can bring me up to speed on that eco-resort in the Philippines."

"If I get in bed with you, we will not be discussing architecture. I doubt we will be talking at all and you're too weak for that kind of activity."

"Of course I'm not weak. Especially if I let you do all the work," she said, wriggling her feathery brows. "I know you long for a wife who will willingly put up with whatever you do to her."

"That sounds like *your* fantasy, *pethi mou*. Not mine."

"What do you think I'm trying to tell you without actually saying it?"

"Maybe I won't understand until you beg me."

"You're mean."

"You're the one who called me names in front of my family. Now even they believe I'm a villain."

He didn't add that his mother already thought so. It hurt him, this unspoken rift between him and his mother, but he had no idea how to fix it. Until recently, he hadn't even wanted to. Though now, he saw that his restlessness of the past few years stemmed also from this disconnection between him and them.

Mama didn't understand his point of view and he definitely didn't understand hers. Neither did he forget that, in Mama's eyes, marrying Jia without knowing his nefarious intentions, which he was now glad Jia hid from her, was the only right thing he had done in his adult life.

"I'm sorry for that," Jia said, flushing. Rocking back and forth on the balls of her feet. "I…overreacted. I'll explain it to them. I'll tell them the antibiotics made my brain wonky. I'll tell them you're the best husband I could've ever asked for, that you keep me well stocked in orgasms. At least, until two weeks ago."

His destruction, he'd never thought, could come in the form of a woman. Or that he would willingly walk toward it. "Not enough," he said, bracing himself against her warmth as she pressed a kiss on his chest.

She stomped her foot and blew impatiently at a lock of hair that dared to caress her cheek. "I miss you, Apollo. Won't you please keep me company?"

He tucked his hands into his pockets, to stop himself from reaching for her. "Not nearly enough."

She exhaled roughly. "I miss…talking with you about work and our vision for the future and I… I miss your kisses and how you let me use you as a squishy when I'm deep in sleep and I'm horny for you and only you. I kept having these feverish dreams where I'm caught under you and I'm not even trying to get away as you have your way with me and those weird dreams were the only thing that made it worth staying in bed. So, my dear husband, won't you please pin me under you and have your wicked way with me?"

Apollo had no idea if she'd said anything past that or if he'd replied at all, because all he could hear was the thundering whoosh of his desire in his ears and all he could feel was the weight of her slender body in his arms as he carried her up to their bedroom.

CHAPTER EIGHT

IT WAS LONG past midnight and Jia thought her bones might crumble to dust if she so much as moved her little finger. But even sated to the point of exhaustion, she couldn't fall asleep.

Apollo had been extra ruthless and demanding and insatiable since she'd slowly been gaining her strength back. There had been a near-frenzy to how he had made love to her, as if he had to make up for the time they had lost when she had been ill. As if he had worried about losing her.

Which was ridiculous because it had been an infection. Even that looked like a blessing given it had shifted something between them. Within her.

Admitting to the promise Mom had asked of her had provided a strange relief and rearrangement of facts in her head. After so many years, she thought of those days when Mom had been sick and everyone had been devastated and Jia had been at the center of the storm. She wondered how confused and scared her mom must have been to extract such a promise from a thirteen-year-old.

Had she ever truly loved Jia? Or had she only seen her as one mistake that she had to make up for, for the rest of her life?

It had taken Apollo's relentless probing to make her question the patterns that had been set a decade ago.

Now this new experience of intimacy with him. A whole week of glutting on him, and not just sex either. He had taught her how to play chess in bed and she had taught him how to binge-watch reality shows—though the workaholic that he was didn't have a natural talent for it. They worked briefly on some design modifications because Apollo had shockingly enough taken the week off, talked about the charity projects he had put aside a decade ago because he hadn't the resources to see them through.

He demanded so much from her that she could imagine living in a different galaxy where *she* was the sun and he some orbiting planet. No one had ever wanted to know how she'd gotten every scar on her body, the meaning of her tattoos, or what her deepest dreams were and why she kept them locked tight.

One evening, he'd flown them to visit a large, and by that she meant *vast*, plot of land that he had bought two days prior.

He was building a new house there and would like her input for its design, he'd murmured when Jia had prodded him through sleep-heavy lids. Irritatingly enough, she had tired far too soon on their outing and had been almost drifting to sleep. Now she had

a feeling he'd whispered the truth because he had
thought her out of it.

A house for their family.

It was a commitment she'd never expected from
this relationship, never dreamed of from this marriage
when she'd broken into his penthouse in New York.

The prospect of that dream, of letting herself see
that far into the future, made her heart dance far too
fast in her chest, coated her skin with slick sweat.

God, despite her best intentions to safeguard her
heart, she wanted it all. To belong to him, to build
a new life with him, to root herself to him and the
house he wanted to build for them…meant hoping
and wishing and praying that he would always want
her with the same intensity. That he would always see
the value in having her in his life. That someday, he
wouldn't see a mistake when he looked at her, like
her Mom always had.

And that kind of faith in him and herself… Jia
didn't know how to build it, much less hold on to it.
She'd never been shown how.

When her rational mind showed her the prospect
of leaving him behind one day, as if to protect her,
her heart raced. Her limbs shook. She pushed herself up on her elbow, to better drink in his haughty,
rough-hewn features.

His dark hair was graying at the temples and his
mouth, relaxed in his sleep, was lush and wide. The
column of his throat, the defined musculature of his
chest and abdomen, everything about him screamed

hardness. And yet, he could be so incredibly tender with her.

In sleep, he looked like the man he'd buried deep under his motives and ambition, the man who hadn't deserted her for a minute when she'd been sick. The man who would do anything for his family but somehow found himself outside of the tight unit.

Jia hadn't missed the distinction.

His mother and sisters loved him and yet, she'd sensed the painful rift, especially between his mother and Apollo. And ever since she'd caught snippets of its source, she finally saw beyond the machinations and the thirst for power to the tormented man beneath it all. Her heart ached with the need to take away his burden, to make him see what kind of man he was outside of this revenge that had consumed two decades of his life.

Giving in to the urge, she traced the bridge of his nose with the tip of her finger and then the bow-shaped curve of his upper lip.

Such little expectations of the people around you, he had said, mocking her.

And it had been easy to follow that edict. Except now, with him. Beneath his obvious anger toward her brother and father, beneath his very righteous belief that here was another way her father was a villain, had been something else though. Something more.

It was such a tempting illusion that Jia fell back against the bed, shaking.

A large, rough palm landed on her belly before

long fingers traced the curve of her hip with a possessive familiarity that made her breath come in little pants. "Not tired enough for sleep?"

"I'm…restless tonight." She was standing at a crossroads, and her heart wanted to go one way and her mind another. One way lay the rational, no-risk, empty life she'd always lived and the other way…lay the possibility of infinite happiness. "Confused," she added, feeling this uncharacteristic urge to bare all of herself to him.

"About?" he said, a grave tone to the single word.

"About myself, you. And us." Each word ripped her out from under all the shackles she had bound herself with. Released her into a new terrifying world. But she couldn't stay put anymore, not after tasting this joy with Apollo.

"What about us?" He practically growled the words at her.

"Why do you want to build another house when we can live in this one?"

"It's a fresh start." He replied readily enough that she knew he had been thinking of it too. "For us."

Or a fresh start for him?

The words he didn't say danced between them, shocking Jia with their vulnerability.

Because this house was tainted with his need to prove something to the world? Because it was tied to the shadow of a man he had not let go of? Because he was finding himself in a new place with her, and wanted to let go of old things like revenge and reparation?

Excitement skittered through her. "If I sign over my stock in my father's company to you tomorrow, instead of three years later as he and you agreed on, will this all be over?"

Delaying the stock transfer was the one thing her father had asked of her when Apollo had given her ten minutes to leave. The one thing she'd promised herself she'd never do.

And yet here she was, ready to betray the man who had raised her.

He only raised you. He wasn't really a father.

She heard the cruel words in Apollo's voice.

The idea took root in her head and was already spreading its gnarled whispers all over, solidifying. What if she could give Apollo what he wanted and this was over? What if it meant a real fresh start for the both of them, and not just a shiny new house? What if it meant there were no conditions hanging over their relationship?

Behind her, Apollo stiffened. Sudden tension swathed them, as if forming their very own bubble. "What?"

"It would bring you controlling percentage in the company, yeah?"

"Yes."

"It's what you wanted all along?"

"Yes."

"If you promise that—"

"He will never forgive you."

"Someday, he will realize that I protected him, that I did only what was best for them. But for now, it will be over."

"He will never realize that, never give you what you're seeking."

"What I choose to believe is my prerogative, *ne*?" she said, imitating his gruff tone. "So, tell me, will it be over?"

"Will what be over?"

"Your…revenge. This pursuit of his destruction."

"You're not signing your stock over to me. What I want will be mine, soon."

"Yes, we've established that, Apollo. And really, I'm just…"

"Just what, *agapi*?"

"I'm thinking of what I want my life to look like in a few years. Thinking of what *I want* for the first time," she said, giving free rein to the emotions sitting like a tight fist at the center of her chest. It was easier when she wasn't looking into that unfathomable gray gaze and wondering if she'd one day drown. "I haven't ever, you know. Thought about what I want, where I want to live, how I want to work and—"

"Let me know when you figure out the specifics."

"Why?"

"So that I can give it to you."

Jia shivered at the steely resolve in those words. Apparently, there was no doubt in his head that he wanted to be married to her for the distant future.

She didn't know what to make of that certainty. Was this chemistry and compatibility enough for him? Did he truly think they could last a lifetime with their pasts so murkily tangled and their foundation built on a cold arrangement? "That's an ambitious promise," she finally said, running her fingers over the coarse hair on this forearm.

His laughter spread ripples on the back of her neck. "You married a man for whom nothing is impossible. I thought you understood your commitment to me."

She could feel his frown like a burn on her cheek as he fully turned toward her, almost angry that her emotions, and she, dared to not follow his dictates. And that made her smile. Because underneath all the ruthless bluster and grumpy dictates, her husband hid a heart of gold.

One hairy, muscled leg thrown over hers, he pulled her closer, and his mouth descended to her neck. That spot where once he kissed her, she lost all reason and logic and self-preservation.

She arched her neck as his teeth grazed the sensitive spot, dampness blooming between her thighs, as easily as if flipping a switch.

"All this talk of your restlessness has made me restless. Only one thing would cure it," he said, each word pinging over her skin.

"It's always only one thing with you," she said, stretching into his touch.

"I want to be inside you," he said, laving the bite

with his tongue. Breathing the words into her skin. "Now. Say yes, *agapi*. *Parakalo*."

When Jia might have turned toward him, he stopped her, one arm crisscrossing between her bare breasts, and the other hand coasting down her side, waist to hip to thigh, finger slowly creeping across her lower belly. Tiny trembles began to skitter across her flesh like ripples on water.

"You're distracting me and it won't…" she whispered, but the thought never fully formed as he dipped his fingers into her folds.

She jerked as he pinched her clit, and traced every inch of her aching flesh until her wetness coated his fingers, and then he told her how it felt when he was inside of her, and how she clenched tight when she thought he might retreat, and how he thought it couldn't get better when he came inside of her but it did. Every single time, it got better.

Words and fingers and lips…he used them all to drive her out of her skin.

She wanted to protest—she wanted to talk to him—but God, the man was enormously talented and Jia moaned as he speared her with two fingers.

"I don't like it when you don't fall in with my plans, wife."

"You don't want a wife. You want a doll who'll play along and be your… Oh."

His mouth was at her nipple, licking, sucking and nipping. Jia had never lost a battle this willingly and this fast.

"No, Tornado," he said, withdrawing his fingers, leaving her empty, lost. "I want *you*, only you, willing and happy and amenable to my plans."

"Come inside me, Apollo," she said, those words propping her up for now, "and I will fall in with any plans, please."

As if all he'd needed was her assent, he lifted her leg and probed her wanton, wet flesh with the head of his cock and then he was thrusting into her from behind and Jia thought she might be the exploding sun itself.

It was a sore, tight fit with a delicious burn in this position but she didn't want to be anywhere else. She didn't want anything else. She felt engulfed by him and she loved it.

Hands kneading and cupping her flesh all over, keeping her still and soft for his tender assault, Apollo set a merciless rhythm, pounding into her. The slap of their flesh, the erotic tussle of their breaths, the words he whispered into her skin…pleasure suffused every inch of her. Their bodies slipped and slid together as if made for each other, racing toward a pinnacle she'd want again and again.

It was only after their climaxes nearly broke them that Jia realized she'd tried to put everything on the line for him. And he hadn't wanted it.

CHAPTER NINE

SHE CAME TO him at dawn, dressed in a thick robe that hung off one smooth shoulder and fell to her ankles. *His robe.*

He hadn't been hiding precisely. But after he had tired her out, desperate to control her, own her, bind her to him, whatever restlessness had chased her seemed to have transferred to him.

It was her offer to sign over her stock to him. Mere weeks ago, the same offer would have been a prize he'd counted as his final win. Now, with his feelings all twisted up about her and his own part in where they were, it felt like a…curse. A gut punch.

Even as he'd lain there boneless and sated, her offer had niggled and pricked.

Why had she offered that to him when it was the only thing of any value she possessed? Did she crave her freedom so much? Was it such a chore to be married to him? What was there for her back in New York except a family that would chew her up for all she was worth and spit her out given half the chance?

He had felt unsettled enough, unwanted enough

that he found it unbearable to stay near her for one more second. For all she tried to buy her way out of his life, she clung to him in sleep, her legs and arms all coiled around him.

That feeling of not being enough struck some deep, primal part of him that he had forgotten existed.

It was the same thing that had haunted him after he'd found Papa unmoving, the same thing he'd tried to escape by pouring himself into climbing the corporate ladder high enough to own it.

And yet, after all that he'd done to get to this place now, that he could once again be haunted by that feeling…threw him. He wanted to run from it, hide from it, go back into bed and work himself out on Jia until they were both exhausted again and she made no foolish offers to get away.

But he was not a fool, and he knew not to outrun the same problem in the same way all over again.

So he was sitting at his desk in the large airy study, the oncoming dawn a distant pink splash in the horizon. For a moment, he considered telling her to leave him alone. But the words stalled, drowned out by his need to hold her, to have her near.

"You need your sleep," he said, tempering his tone somehow, intensely disliking the knowledge that he could hurt her with one wrong word.

It was a dangerous power to have, because he hadn't met a kind that he didn't wield in the end. Not even Mama's utter dislike of him had broken his taste for it, once he'd had it.

Hands clamped on the sash of the robe, she walked to him, instantly fitting herself in between his legs, as if she belonged there.

"You're not happy about my offer." She pushed her hair behind her ear, confusion writ in her gaze. Her frown cleared. "No, you're angry about my offer. Why?"

He looked past her and the glass wall into the inky night beyond. Every memory today seemed to bring him back to the helplessness he'd struggled with after Papa's death. *Dios mio*, he'd had many sleepless nights, just like this. "What's your condition for it?"

"Are you sure that I have one?" Her expression was somber now.

He nodded.

"Finish this revenge of yours. Let them be. Let yourself be."

He scoffed. "I should've known."

Her eyes flashed but she corralled her temper and it was a sight to behold. "Rina told me earlier that Vik *is* facing the consequences. She's moving in with her chauffeur. With you having controlling stock, my father can't afford the delusion anymore that he can come back from this. He has lost everything, Apollo. You have won. So let it be," she said, clasping his cheeks and tugging until he looked down at her. Her eyes were wide, brimming with an emotion he couldn't read. "I ask it for you too. So that you can be free."

He pulled away from her so fast that she almost

stumbled. But he caught her, then released her. "I do not need any favors, Jia," he said, stubbornly. "At least nothing that's not part of our deal."

She joined him at the chaise longue, hands folded primly in her lap. "I have spent enough time with your family to realize that your father's death wasn't… a natural one. To understand that your need to pay for his loss has caused a rift between you and your mother. I know you enough to see that this revenge has cost you even more than it has cost my father."

"Sleeping with me for a few weeks doesn't make you an expert on me."

If he thought she'd be hurt, he was wrong. Her chin tilted up, a combative expression entering her eyes. "And yet you were right about me. You made me doubt if my mom even saw me as anything but a mistake she had to make up for. You made me wonder if she molded me into this…pushover for the rest of my family as part of her reparation to him. You made me realize that maybe he never truly loved me as he did Rina or Vik. If the mind-blowing orgasms you dole out have given you that much insight into me, why shouldn't I have the same?" She smiled then, and it was the most breathtaking sight Apollo had ever seen. His chest ached to be in its presence and ached more anticipating its absence. "Plus, like you said, your sisters are blunt and voluble."

He clasped her cheek, the need to touch her ever present. "Is it me you want to free from the past or yourself from the present?" The words fluttered between them, dripping with his vulnerability.

She frowned. "I don't understand."

Her confusion was genuine enough that some deep longing in him settled. "If you think I'll release you from this marriage because you sign over your stock—"

"I didn't think that," she said, tapping the side of her head. "After all, as we both know, the real asset is my brain. At least, until you're addicted to my body—and my mouth," she said, licking her lower lip, "and then that becomes the real asset."

He grinned, suddenly feeling light as a feather. It was another new feeling in the box he was collecting of them. And the realization that maybe, just maybe, she truly meant for him to be free, as well as her own father, filled him with awe and that dissonance again.

What did he do with such a woman? He was running out of deals and conditions and contracts that he could use to bind her.

He sat down on the chaise longue next to her and she instantly leaned her head against his shoulder, utterly unaware of how her every touch and kiss and caress unmanned him. "Is it true that you…found him?"

"He was cold when I touched his hand."

She took his hand and laced their fingers and clasped him so tight that he felt the crust of ice around his heart melt. He hadn't talked about this with a single soul, not even Mama. And suddenly the words came easy, as if all these years, they'd been waiting to be released. "I was…so angry in those first moments. I could only think of myself and how he had abandoned me when I worshipped him. He was my hero. That he didn't think I, or any of us, were enough to hold on to, to find a way to move forward. And the only way I could escape that feeling was to channel all that rage into action, toward the right man."

"I can't imagine how hopeless he must have felt after losing so much. But he did abandon you, Apollo. It's okay to love him and still be angry with him over that." When he let her words soothe him, she scoffed. "Says the woman who craves her father's approval even though she knows she'll never get it," she added with a flippancy.

"All I have fed for nearly two decades is that rage and it has burned everything else down. I'm a stranger to my own family. Mama has never understood that rage, that drive to make your father pay, the need to amass so much power and wealth that no one can ever make me feel like that again."

Only to learn now that no power or wealth could buy him this woman's loyalty.

"But you're here now, with them," she said, coming into his lap like Camilla's cat, demanding to be pet, and vined herself around him. "And you could begin again. All they want is a word from you to build that bridge. All they want is to know that the boy they know and love is still there beneath the ruthless billionaire."

Apollo didn't miss the wistful note in her words

and tightened his arms around her. Neither did he miss the fact that his mother's sudden approval of him was mostly due to this complex creature he had married, which had come about by her design and his greed. The fact that his fate could have been so much worse didn't sit well with his need for control.

"So what do you think of my offer? Can you get the paperwork ready?"

"No," he said instinctively, without even examining the source of it. "I don't want to take those stock options away from you. Not yet," he added to keep her dangling.

"But that means you still—"

"Leave it, Jia. You have solved enough problems for him."

"I told you, Apollo. This isn't about him."

"Excuse me if I don't believe that you can break the pattern of a lifetime in a moment, *agapi*."

Within a blink of an eye, she was out of his arms and halfway across the study, fury radiating from her.

"You're being childish," he called out, wanting to chase her and pin her down under him like a predator. He was beginning to feel like that was all he'd want for the rest of his life. To have her writhing under him, biting at him with her tart words, softening in those moments when she let down her armor enough to trust him.

Her eyes glowed in the soft light of the lamp as she halted at the doorway. "If you want us to be locked in this…arrangement forever, fine." She was almost out when she paused, her throat bobbing up and down. "But then I want nothing to do with the house you build. I'm not leaving this house and I'm definitely not starting a…"

Whatever she saw in his eyes, she swallowed the rest of her words. Something unbearably sad flashed across her face before she turned away.

Apollo thought she might have said, *So much for a fresh start for you and me.* But he was damned if he begged her to explain any more than he already had. Or stay in his life willingly. He had already cornered himself into a weaker position and the uncertainty of it picked at him night and day.

He had married her as part of the deal she herself had struck and he would be a poor businessman if he let her change the terms of their deal now. And he wasn't done with her father, as she had so naively assumed.

CHAPTER TEN

JIA WALKED UP to the second-floor open terrace that looked out into the turquoise sea and took in a deep breath of fresh air on the unseasonably warm day. It did little to calm her stomach that afternoon.

She'd been feeling queasy all day but she'd kept it to herself. Apollo, with his usual bullheadedness, would've sent her back to bed and she'd miss seeing the house that his firm had custom-designed and nearly finished for a seventy-year-old Arab tycoon.

It was the first house they'd designed together. Granted, near to completing it, Apollo had been stuck in some aspects and Jia had helped make a few modifications. And now, there it stood carved into the side of a hill. The expanse of blue sea and green hillside working perfectly to encapsulate the all-white home.

Jia wasn't usually a fan of the modern contemporary designs that lacked all warmth and color, and rejected natural elements like wood and fabric. Solely depending on steel and chrome, they looked like geometric cubes.

But here, in this house, the sharp, flat cube design had no flourishes. Only white walls and glass, which served to highlight the lush, natural landscape around it. A rectangular pool at the front of the house reflected sunlight like jewels on its blue surface.

It was a perfect escape for anyone who wanted to get away from the hustle, the perfect destination for a small family to spend the weekend. God, she was beginning to think like Apollo Galanis's wife, with thoughts of summer homes and island destinations. When she didn't have a single nickel to her name.

It had never bothered her before. All she'd lived for was to win her family's approval, to somehow contribute to their well-being. Only last week, she'd learned that the stock she owned in her father's company had shot up meteorically. Not unconnected to the formal press release that Apollo Galanis was taking over the firm.

Weeks after she'd made the offer to sign it over to him, Jia still didn't understand why he didn't take her up on it. How long could she bear to have the shadow of the past color their relationship?

Joy tingled on her lips when he kissed her, danced through her body when he made love to her, was beginning to shine like a flame in her chest when he looked through a crowd or coworkers or his family for her. When he spotted her, those little crinkles appeared at the corners of his eyes and his mouth curled up. Everything around them dissolved, leaving the two of them alone in the entire universe.

Even knowing the truth of the trauma Apollo had

faced when he'd discovered his father's body and everything that had followed, Jia couldn't find it in herself to hurt her father anymore. If that made her a sentimental pushover, so be it. It wasn't like she was faring any better with Apollo. In a mere two months, she had shifted her loyalty to him without any qualms.

Absentmindedly, she took a sip of the champagne. It coated her throat with a slick bile, threatening to bring up the little she'd managed to eat at breakfast. Bad enough that her period was due any day now and…

Jia quickly checked her calendar. Shock jostled her stomach a little more as she looked at the colorful numbers. She'd had only one period since she'd arrived in Greece and that was nearly nine weeks ago, when they'd still been in Athens. Her legs trembled as she came down the stairs to the main level.

Was she pregnant?

Having a baby with Apollo was the last thing she'd ever imagined, when she'd struck the deal with him. But the thought of not having the baby filled her throat with fresh bile and she nearly tripped on the way to the bathroom.

Large hands held her hair back as she emptied her stomach, whispering reassurances, holding her when her knees buckled.

Jia washed up, doing her best to avoid looking at the large circular mirror and meeting his watchful eyes. If she did, he would know. And if Apollo knew, he would be…happy. She knew that as surely as her racing heartbeat.

A house for us and the family we might have.

Closing her eyes, Jia leaned into the hard warmth of his body behind her. His corded forearm clasped around her waist with utter gentleness. "I'll have the chopper ready in five minutes. You should have told me you weren't feeling well."

Tears filled Jia's eyes and she trembled with the effort to hold them back. She'd have to take a pregnancy test, yes, but she knew. Especially since she'd been told that antibiotics could mess with the pill.

Slowly, shock gave way to crystal-clear clarity.

"What's wrong, *agapi*? Where does it hurt?" Apollo said in a voice she'd never heard from him.

But she couldn't say anything because the thing she did want to say was the biggest truth of her life. She wanted to stand at the highest peak, and scream into the sea and the sky that she had fallen in love with him.

She was in love with her husband. And with this baby, *their baby*, which was probably no bigger than the size of a tiny worm right then.

And she was in love with how precious their life together that he kept showing her tiny, taunting glimpses of, could be.

She was in love with a man who was obsessed with making her father pay for his sins and in the process, refused to feel anything else, a man who considered her an asset. A man who in the pursuit of that revenge had even alienated his own mother.

"Jia, look at me. *Parakalo*."

It was the *please* that did it, full of his own desperation, that reminded her that he did care for her, but just not in the way she wanted him to.

She turned around and threw herself at him and cried like she'd never done before. How could he be the storm that was wrecking her and still also be the only harbor left to her?

God, she couldn't bear the weight of loving Apollo without him loving her back. She didn't want to spend the rest of her life locked in a marriage with a man who would always see her last name first, or her brains and now the fact that she was his child's mother.

Would he ever want her for herself, even as he built castles for their now very real family? Would he love her as she longed to be loved, as she loved him?

And if she stayed, she would be trapped and miserable, unable and unwilling to give him up. But could she leave him and raise this baby alone? Would he even let her? Or would she be ruining a bright present in search of a future that didn't exist?

"Enough, Jia," Apollo was whispering into her temple, his hands moving over her back in a frenzy, a rough bite to his words. "You will make yourself sick and I will not allow it. Enough, *agapi mou*. Whatever it is, I will fix it."

The scent of him filled her lungs and instantly her

body calmed, as if it knew him better than her mind did. Even better than her heart.

Jia clung to him, took solace in his words, even though she knew it was only temporary. "I'm scared, Apollo. I…"

"Of what, Jia?"

She buried her face in his neck—her safe space. Here, she could feel his steady pulse and breathe in the pine and clove scent, and know that with those arms around her, she wouldn't be lost.

His hands moved over her, kneading and pressing, gathering her so tight to him that she felt like she might break apart. His mouth was at her temple, warm and soft. "Shh… Tornado. You're with me and I won't let you go."

And when he lifted her in his arms, and walked through the house that he'd built and carried her to the roof in front of all the staring guests as if she were precious, as if nothing else mattered, Jia wondered if she could be brave enough to do the one thing she'd never done in her entire life.

For Apollo, could she hope? For this baby and the life they might build together, could she trust in herself that she was worthy of his love? Could she stay and love him as she wanted to?

Apollo watched Jia as she half-heartedly riffled through the design folders he'd brought in from the firm, at her request. From playing video games with Camilla's sons to cooking with his mother, to her work, everything she did these days was with half a heart, her mind a million miles away.

Something was wrong, ever since that day two weeks ago when they'd been visiting a client's home in Andros Island. He had never seen such panic in Jia's eyes and even now, if he closed his eyes, her expression haunted him.

To this day, she wouldn't tell him what had made her cry as if her heart was breaking.

Oh, she pretended that everything was good, but he caught that haunted look in her eyes when she thought he wasn't watching or when she forgot to keep her armor up. He also didn't miss how her moods fluctuated from happiness to sudden sadness, like a shroud dimming her spirit.

The only place where he had her completely, where he knew only his touch ruled her, was in bed. She was as desperate to be touched and held and consumed as she'd been before and if it wasn't for that intimacy that tethered her to him, he might have lost his mind by now.

He was getting there slowly though, seeing the constant shadow in her eyes, wondering what he could do to fix it, wondering how he could get the old Jia back.

He'd even hounded Rina about the cause, wondering if her family was at the root of her problems, as always. Rina had not only come up empty, but finally showed a little backbone by asking him if he'd considered that he could be the source of Jia's pain.

Jia married you because she had no choice, Rina had pointed out, with sudden acidity, and the doubt had been planted.

Jia was unhappy with him, with their relationship, and he had no idea how to fix it, for all he'd promised her he would. Asking her had got him nothing but evasion.

I've given you everything, Apollo. There's nothing left, had been Jia's sarcastic taunt when he'd probed. And then, like a child seeking approval from an adult they'd alienated, she had clung to him that night.

"You're worried about her."

Apollo turned to find his mother next to him, holding up a cup of dark coffee in one hand. Just the scent of it told him she'd prepared it the exact way he liked it. The realization arrested his childish impulse to snub her offer.

He hadn't even been aware of her presence in the kitchen, so caught up he was in watching Jia. For once, all his sisters and their broods were busy elsewhere and the house was eerily quiet.

With nothing else to do, he took the coffee mug and turned away.

"Will you not talk to me, Apollo?" Mama said, her words heartbreakingly soft.

He shrugged, a sudden patina of grief and anger clinging to his throat. For so long, they had been at odds with each other. She had been critical of everything he had done, and he hadn't cared enough to mend the direction of his life. And now, when he'd achieved everything he'd set out to own, when the world was at his feet, this rift with his mother was still an open wound.

Was it too late to mend it? Did he even want to?

The moment the resentful thought came, he found the answer. Of course he wanted to build a bridge to his mother again. But he didn't know how. Just as he didn't know how to help Jia.

"I'm still your mother, Apollo, even if you have conquered the entire world," she said, rebuking him with the same thoughts.

She came to stand next to him and her subtle sandalwood perfume came to him. A river of longing opened up, touched by memories of baking with her in a tiny kitchen, of hugging her and feeling so secure, of…seeing her strong face break into terrible sobs when she'd seen Papa's body, of how long she'd spoken to him that night about how it wasn't his fault. That Papa had loved them all, but he hadn't been strong enough.

"You tried very hard that evening, after I…found him," he said.

She frowned, an instant shadow of grief touching her eyes. A long sigh then. "You were always your Papa's son. I knew how much you adored him and I also understood how betrayed you must have felt. Because I felt the same."

The mug clattered onto the tiled counter with enough noise to wake the dead, but across the open space, sitting in the living room, staring at something in the distance, Jia didn't even stir.

Apollo pressed the heels of his palms into his eyes, the past and present combining and separating as if in a science fiction movie—one Jia had made him watch. "I felt so…helpless and angry."

His mother, so tiny and small beside him, wrapped her arm around his waist and squeezed. "I wish I had helped you in a better way to—"

"No, Mama. You were right when you said that he could have been stronger for us. None of us wanted the wealth he lost or needed it. We would have moved into a hut with him and still been happy. He didn't see that, didn't realize the value of that and I…" his breath came in shallow pants "… I chose a path that made me lose you too."

"But you have not lost me, or your sisters, Apollo," she said, her voice steely in its resolve. "We have all been here, waiting for you. And you haven't lost the kindness that was so much a part of your Papa's either. All the good parts are still there."

"I am not so sure."

Mama covered his hand on the countertop. "You're admitting defeat, Apollo?"

He laughed and examined his hands. "I'm admitting that everything I have done so that I never feel helpless again…doesn't work. All the wealth, all the power I have amassed are no use to me when I want to…"

"What?" Mama said, following his gaze to the

woman in the living room. The woman he realized held his heart in her slender, tender hands. "Tell me."

"Something is wrong with her."

It came to him slowly, as if he was moving through a fog, that his mother wasn't surprised. "In what way?"

"She smiles but there's a shadow. She talks but it's different. She clings to me at night, but it's as if she's running away from some great sorrow. She will not tell me what it is and I'm afraid that she's slipping from my fingers. I'm afraid that there is nothing in the world that I can do to fix this for her."

"I have seen what you speak of, Apollo. She's quieter than she usually is. Maybe she's homesick?"

Apollo turned so fast that his neck hurt. "Did she say that to you?"

"She has been talking a lot about families and how they come to be. She asked if I had been happy with your father. She's been begging Camilla and Christina to talk about children and families and how they knew if they were ready."

Was that simply it, that she missed her damned family?

"I wondered if she…"

"She, what?" When his mother hesitated, Apollo grabbed her hand. "I'm going mad trying to figure this out."

Her soft gaze lit on his face, carefully scrutinizing every inch. "Why?"

"Why what?"

"Why are you so worried?"

"Because I've pulled her away from her entire world, her family, her friends and she's mine. Because I…"

Because he was in love with her and he would do anything to make the world right for her again. Except let her go, he added to himself.

Maybe it wasn't love, then. Maybe it was something else. Maybe it was his need to control this too. Wasn't love supposed to be selfless and grand and divine?

He felt the opposite, like there was a storm brewing in his stomach. Like he'd never know certainty in anything ever again.

"Please, Mama."

"I wondered if she…" hesitation danced in her eyes "…is pregnant."

It felt like he had been slapped so hard that the echoes of it rang in his ears. Every inch of him stilled.

"When Camilla asked gently, she said you two are not planning for a family and…"

The rest of his mother's words drifted away as Apollo moved past her to the stairs. He took them three at a time, his heart thrashing around in his chest like a crushed toy.

All her stuff lay in half-open cosmetic bags or in haphazard piles in the drawers in the bathroom. He rifled through her handbag and her jewelry box and her pen case and her…

He found the discarded pill sheet first, sitting innocently under a pile of underwear. And in another drawer, a pharmacy receipt for two pregnancy tests. He didn't have to see the tests themselves to know that his mother's guess was right.

Jia had been sick that day when they'd been touring the client's house in Andros Island, had had no appetite for days after and she had been so panic-stricken because she… She was pregnant.

With his child.

Their child.

A child she'd never planned for, and had made it clear enough times that she didn't want with him. A child whose very conception had made her sick at heart. A child she was keeping a secret from him, over whom she was turning herself into a shadow.

Did she hate the idea so much, enough to want to…leave him?

It felt like a crack reverberated through his heart, the thought was that painful.

And in that moment of utter confusion and anguish, Apollo knew. In that moment when he had to face the possibility that Jia wanted to leave him, he knew.

It was as solid and real as the house he had built for his mother. As real as the anger he had finally allowed himself to feel against his father for abandoning them. As real as the hope he'd been nurturing for weeks now.

Dios mio, he was in love with his wife and he had no idea how to sit with that knowledge. When he knew that she was only in his life because he had forced her hand. When he knew that anything they had shared, anything they had created together, like this precious child, had been an accident of his path, not her choice.

He sank to the floor and clutched his head in his hands, feeling like he had hit the bottom of the world. Still, the crash was unending. But even through the panic pulsing through him, there was a pinprick of awe at this new emotion swirling through him.

He was in love and he had never known anything more terrifying or more wonderful.

CHAPTER ELEVEN

THREE WEEKS AFTER her discovery, Jia had come up with a hundred different plans for how she could tell Apollo and discarded them all. Her period had always thrashed her about like a ship caught in a storm, and it seemed her pregnancy was going to be more of the same. Despite that, she'd forced herself to consider the ugly prospect of leaving him with a clear mind.

What kind of a future would she be providing for her child? Apollo had helped her shed her rose-colored lenses about her family. She would be all alone in the world with a tiny precious baby to care for.

That was, assuming Apollo simply let her go.

Abandoning his pregnant wife was something he would never do.

And if she stayed…would things get better? Could her love simply wither and die if she didn't nurture it? Could she one day forget that it even existed, flickering like a live flame inside her chest? Would it be so bad to make a family with him knowing he admired her, respected her, even cared for her, in his own way?

When the questions became too much, she floated through her days in a strange limbo. Like a flesh wound on her finger hidden away under layers of gauze, so she only felt it when she had to use it. Then it became a pulsing throb of pain.

Nights were easier to get through.

Especially like now, when she was in bed and waiting for Apollo to join her. She'd spent the whole day with so many doubts that all she wanted was his brand of possession.

In the dark intimacy of their bedroom, she forgot everything. In their bed, with his hard, warm body tangled around hers or pinning her down into the mattress as he drove them to sweet release, or as he cradled her from behind and drowned her in his caresses making sweet love to her, it was easy to imagine that Apollo adored her as much as she adored him.

A sudden ping on her phone had her scooting up on the bed. It was a text from her sister.

Reading it made tears prick her eyelids—what didn't these days?—and laugh at the same time. But beneath the joy that Rina was getting married and the acceptance of her sister's long, heartfelt apology, a dark envy lingered. If Rina, who'd always let their father and brother intimidate her, who'd never gone against the grain even in thought, could find true love, why couldn't Jia?

With uncharacteristic frustration, Jia threw her cellphone across the bedroom. It landed with a loud thump on the rug. God, what was she turning into? It was almost as if the pregnancy and her love for Apollo were releasing all the petty and intense but valid emotions she had caged inside all her life.

"Jia?" Apollo stood under the archway to their bedroom. "Did you just throw your phone across the room?"

"Yes."

"Feel better?"

"No."

With moonlight coming in through the glass walls behind him, every angle of him was limned lovingly as if she herself had crafted him with her hands.

A broad chest, strong shoulders, tapering to a thin waist and abdominal muscles that she rubbed herself on without shame…he was everything she'd never even had the nerve to imagine. Just the sight of him made her heart flutter with dizzying pleasure, her body come alive as if it had been sleeping for years.

Powerful and yet kind beneath the grumpy exterior, a man who was a hundred times worthier than the man she called father…

Was he hers? Could he be hers forever? Was her love enough to sustain them?

Suddenly, Jia knew what she had to do. Her happiness, her spark for life, her very joy itself was already bound to this man. How could she leave him? She had spent all her life serving her undeserving family, hoping to earn a smile, a pat, approval from a man who didn't even see her.

How could she do anything less for the man who

had seen her messy, chaotic self from the first moment and only found it fascinating? For the man who had only tried to protect her when he thought she was being harmed, the man who encouraged her to scale new career heights, the man who was always telling her to never dilute her vision, to never lessen herself for anyone, including him?

A sudden rush of energy filled her at her resolution. Her lips curved. Her body thrummed with fresh need that wasn't just about escaping her worries, but with new appreciation, for her own desire and for him.

"Jia?" Apollo said her name again. Only this time, it was heavy with frustration. With...pain even. He thrust a hand through his hair, making it stand up every which way.

Coming to her knees on the bed, Jia extended her hands to him. "Will you hold me, Apollo?"

He threw the towel he'd been holding and reached her in seconds with those long strides. Whatever she'd asked of him, however unreasonable she'd been with her own indecision, he'd held her through it, through the storm, without complaint. Without making her feel like she was a burden.

Even her own mother had thought her a burden at one time.

Jia threw herself at him, shuddering with relief brought on by her decision. It was right. She knew it in her bones.

His skin was warm, his muscles tense and hard as he wrapped those steely arms around her. She laid open-mouthed kisses on his bare chest, leaving little dents with her teeth, loving the rough bristle of his chest hair against her skin. The lacy top she'd worn rasped against her beading nipples, making the torment a thousand-fold.

"You're shaking, *matia mou*," he said, his mouth at her temple. "*Again.* Jia…" her name was both a mantra and a curse on his lips "…this…whatever this is needs to stop. We can't continue…you can't…"

"I know. I know," she said, looking up.

His eyes caught her, trapping her in the midst of a maelstrom. A shaft of fear pierced Jia at what she saw there, even though she couldn't put a name to it.

"I'll do better, Apollo," she said, just as she had once promised her mother, so desperate to please and matter and love. But tonight, this promise to her husband wasn't borne out of that same desperation. This promise was different. It moved through her like a rich, fertile sapling spreading its branches, planting roots deep inside her.

This wasn't just for a reward or for approval or to earn love. As if anyone ever had to.

No, she wanted to make him happy. She wanted to please him, make him laugh, make him see who he was beneath all the layers he'd covered himself in. She wanted to love him as well as he loved her, even if he never said the words.

She stroked her palms over his shoulders, loving the tight stretch of his skin over muscles. Loving that she already knew his flesh so well. "You've been very patient with me and I've been an awful employee and an even more awful wife but I swear I will—"

"You think that's what I care about?" he said, roughly tugging her up, until she looked into his eyes. He looked tormented. Unraveled, like she'd never seen him before. Angry, yes, but afraid too. And she'd never seen that in Apollo's eyes. "That you're not performing at peak efficiency at work? Or that you haven't behaved like however a proper wife is supposed to act? Do you think so little of me, Jia?"

He hadn't raised his voice but there was an edge to it that had her searching his face for answers. Alarm punched through her. He was right.

She'd been like one of those gothic heroines Rina was always reading about, walking around dark, edgy moors with tears running down her cheeks, her hair in a disarray, waiting for someone to save her. But she'd already saved herself, with Apollo by her side.

She just hadn't known it. Worse, she'd been so deep in her head that she hadn't wondered how it must have looked to Apollo. Clearly, he had been paying attention to everything she'd done and not done.

"No, of course not. But I know it's not easy to live with a moping mess of a—"

"So what? How do you plan to suddenly not be that…woman?" His fingers were digging into her shoulders, not hurting but not gentle either. "What magical potion will you take to just transform all of a sudden?"

"I have been thinking of magical potions in the

past week too. One I would sneak into your morning coffee so that I could have my wicked way with you, so I could make you give me everything I want. Whatever I want." She moved her hand between their chests, grinning like a loon. "Made for each other."

The cold frost in his eyes broke, and his mouth twitched. "You are insane."

"I know there's no potion, Apollo. I just made a decision, is all."

His hand snuck under her top, and his palm felt abrasively delicious kneading her hip. "You don't need one with me. You could simply ask."

"And you would give it to me?" she said, feeling feverish and elated.

"Anything."

She rubbed herself up against his chest, and groaned when her nipples peaked to hard points. "Before I tell you how I plan to leave behind that gothic heroine in the making…"

Distracted by the play of his muscles, she ran her finger down his pecs, over his hard stomach and over the seam of his sweatpants, and down, over the shapely outline of his growing cock. Need twanged between her thighs and she rubbed them for relief.

How could she have forgotten how real this heat between them was? How could she have forgotten that they had made this child, *their child*, in an act of complete surrender to each other?

It had to have been that afternoon after she'd barely recovered. When she'd screamed murder at him and he'd solved her problems for her in the flicker of a second. When he'd carried her to their bed in the middle of the afternoon and coaxed her to drink her soup and then made love to her as if he'd been starved for her. With the afternoon sun warming their already damp skin, it was the first time Jia had wondered about a future with him.

How could she have even imagined for a second separating him from their child?

"Jia?"

She looked up, colored at his scrutiny and went for his lips. He grunted with surprise when she bit his lower lip, nearly drawing blood and then when he let her in, she kissed him roughly, chasing his tongue, letting him take all her breath and her beats and all of her want. All the things she wanted to say to him and couldn't, she poured into her kiss, hoping he would understand, hoping he would see how crazy she was about him.

His fingers tightened in her hair as he took control of the kiss. And the tenor of it only intensified.

He was angry, Jia realized as he nipped at her lower lip. He gripped her jaw with tight fingers holding her just so for his assault, then dragged his teeth down her jawline and over the arch of her neck, as he came back for her lips like a drowning man reaching for land. Over and over again.

When she gasped out a rough breath, he pulled back. "You're like glass in my hands and I'm being even more rough than usual."

"No," Jia said, grabbing his hand and bringing it to her cheek.

"You have never lied to me before."

"I'm not now," she said, heat streaking her cheeks. "You were rough. But I want rough with you, Apollo. I want whatever brings you to your knees."

Holding his gaze, she cupped his cock and squeezed him over the sweatpants, just the way he liked. A short grunt escaped his mouth before his fingers arrested her roving hand, and tugged it up. She flattened her palm against his chest, and scraped her nails over the taut muscle there, wanting to leave deep gouges in his skin.

God, loving him was making her bloodthirsty.

"Tell me first."

She placed her cheek next to her palm, eager to hear his heartbeat. It was a thundering whoosh against her ears. "I want to feel you move inside me. I want to…lose myself in you."

His fingers were at the nape of her neck, crawling upward and cradling her head. "I cannot believe I'm saying this. But you can't use sex as an escape or as manipulation. Whatever is good about it will be lost then."

She looked up, feeling both shame and shock. "I didn't…" She held her answer as she looked into his eyes. The pain there stole her breath. Had she hurt him? Had she been so blind that she hadn't seen what she was doing to him? "I wasn't using it to escape or to manipulate either of us. I just needed the reassurance that things between us can be good."

"They won't be if you hide from me."

She swallowed at the soft thrust, so close to the truth, and nodded. "I'm trying, Apollo. I really am. I needed to know that there was more than just an arrangement between us. More than—"

"So what suddenly caused the good mood, then?"

She pouted at his commanding tone. "Can't we have sex first, please? And no, I'm not using it for anything. I want to celebrate you and me and…what better way?" When he only continued to consider her with that thick-lashed gaze, she sighed. "I will even go down on you and do that thing I've been preparing to do for three weeks."

"Tempting offer, *agapi*," he said, running his knuckles over the gaping neckline of her top. "But no."

"I just don't want us to fight and then—"

"Then don't do the thing that would make me mad and lead us to fight."

"God, now you sound like the grumpy beast you were when we first met. Fine! At least we can have angry sex then."

"Jia…" he said, elongating her name, telling her he was at the end of his tether.

"Rina's getting married. I want to be there for the wedding."

For just a second, Jia thought she saw him flinch. But why would he?

"When?"

She also had a feeling that his first impulse had been to say no and that he'd barely stopped it. "Next week. God knows where Vik is and my father's definitely not attending. I don't want her to be alone."

"You were alone for our wedding."

"I asked Rina but…"

"Right, you didn't want anyone to see you going under the guillotine, even though it was for them."

"First of all, it was a choice I made. So please stop calling it that. In fact, when things are better, I want to have a different…" God, was it any wonder he was looking at her as if she'd lost her mind? She was doing this all wrong. "I'm not going to spend the rest of my life being bitter about what they have done or not done for me. Especially now that Rina has apologized for 'being naively useless' and wants to start our relationship over. Even my father texted asking how I was, and he never ever texts."

He raised a brow. Jia had the fantastical thought he looked like some apex predator waiting to pounce at the slightest hint of weakness.

"I just want to go for a short trip and I feel like I need to see them and…" Again, she swallowed her words. It was getting harder and harder. There was so much she wanted to tell him but…she knew the timing was wrong. And she needed just a little bit of courage. Courage she was hoping she'd find after one look at her old life. "I'm a little homesick, Apollo. Is that so hard to understand?"

The tension in his features eased just a bit and Jia knew she hadn't imagined his flinch earlier. "We will leave in a couple of days. *If* you continue to be well."

"If I continue... Wait, you...you'll come to New York with me?"

"Is that a problem?"

"You hate my family. If she sees you at the town hall, Rina will probably faint straightaway."

"That's her problem, no?"

"But this is..." She straightened and pulled back, feeling a sudden snap of tension coil around them. Tight enough that her breath shallowed out. "Why does it sound like this trip is conditional on your coming?"

"Why is it conditional if I just want to attend my wife's spoiled sister's wedding?"

Jia fell back on her haunches and stared up at him. There was a curve to his mouth that mocked her. It wasn't a sneer but it was there sure enough. That part of her that was used to going on offense flared up but she fought the impulse.

Something *was* off with him and she had a feeling in her gut that she was responsible for it. And she had this overpowering need to soothe it, to soothe *him*.

"When we left after the wedding, it was in such a hurry. You barely gave me any time and every assumption I made about you, and this marriage and about us...it's been turned upside down. I just...want to see my old home, my family, my life as it was before, with this new lens I have now. I want to say goodbye to my mom for the last time. I..."

Apollo stepped back from the bed, his jaw tightening with each word she said. "You can do all that with me by your side."

The tautly stretched cord snapped. She jumped from the bed, that sudden energy she wanted to use up driving him to the edge, fueling her anger. "This is ridiculous. You do realize that I don't actually need your permission to leave, right?"

"And if I *ask* you to not go without me?"

She threw her hands up in frustration. "Why are you being so...stubborn? I've played along with everything you decided from the moment I stepped into your damned penthouse and I'm truly asking for one thing. One thing for myself, that you already promised me and you're acting as if you don't even trust me to—"

"I don't. I don't trust that you will return."

His words were so hollow that Jia wondered if she was imagining them. But one look at his tight mouth told her she wasn't. Her stomach made an alarming swoop. "You don't trust me to...return? You think I'm using this trip as an excuse to..." She rubbed a hand over her chest. "What? Leave you? Run away from you? How can you say that?"

"You're pregnant. Pregnant with my child, *our child*. And you haven't said a word about it. You've turned yourself inside out, you have made yourself sick, you don't eat, you don't sleep, you...stare up at me with those eyes at night. *Three weeks, Jia!*" The more agitated he became, the quieter his voice got and each word landed like a stone pelting her flesh. "You have known for three weeks and you have made me watch you torment yourself. I've never felt so power-less and this is counting that I found my father's dead body." He drew in a sharp breath, and paced around the bed, like a caged tiger. Tension poured out from every inch of his body. "And now, suddenly, you make this one-eighty today. You tell me things are going to change. You tell me to give you one last thing. How do I know you'll return? How do I know you won't take my growing child with you and disappear? Can you honestly tell me that you didn't consider it for one second?"

Jia opened her mouth and closed it, feeling a cold fist in her chest, spreading like a crack in ice over a lake.

He'd figured it out. Of course he'd figured it out. God, how stupid was she? What had her fear and cowardice brought them to?

Instead of telling him the truth, instead of shar-ing her fears, instead of having faith in the best thing that had ever happened to her, she'd broken the little, tenuous trust that had formed between them. "I did think that. But that's because—"

He flinched, and stepped back. As if she was a thing that could harm and hurt him. And Jia's heart broke alongside his. "And yet you throw it in my face that you don't need my permission? Of course you don't need my permission to go anywhere or to see your damned family. But if you're leaving me, with my child in your belly, have the courage to say it to my face."

"I'd never have run away like that," she said, willing him to hear the conviction in her voice. "Never. But leaving you, yes, I considered it. And discarded it, all in a minute. Not telling you was..." she said, getting off the bed.

He stared at her as she walked toward him as if she was his nightmare come alive.

"Killing me. If you saw the torment, you know the reason now. I wanted to share it with you, I wanted to make plans with you, I wanted to tell you that..."

He clutched her wrists when she wanted to wrap her arms around him, and stared down at her, some dark, hungry thing in his eyes.

It was his faith in her, in them, flickering out, Jia realized, on its last breath. All along, it had been there, brilliant and alive and she had nearly doused it with her fears and foolishness.

"But you did not," he said, releasing her. As if he couldn't bear to touch her. "Every moment of you not telling me, every breath felt like torture. Like torment. And then all of a sudden, you say you have a solution. You say you will be better. You want to leave for bloody New York. What do you think that leads me to believe?"

"I know. And I'm so sorry, Apollo. I wanted that trip to be a goodbye to the old me, the stupid, scared, pushover me. I wanted to come back to our life, to this life with a free, fresh perspective. I wanted to beg my father to—"

"I don't want you to have anything to do with your blasted family."

"I don't want anything from them either," Jia said, her own voice rising now. "Why do you think I've been pushing you to forget about this damned revenge? Why do you think I offered to sell my stock to you even though it was the one thing I swore to myself I wouldn't do?"

"I don't want your stock. I told you—"

"How can you not see how that makes me feel? I wanted you free of this obsession with him, with that company. I wanted us free of the thing that brought us together. I wanted a fresh start with you. And I knew seeing them and my old life would only show me how far I've come. Would give me courage."

He shook his head and Jia knew he wasn't listening. That her hiding the truth had taken him out at the knees. That his feelings for her, the very feelings she'd been afraid he didn't have, made it possible for her to hurt him.

He pressed the heels of his hands to his eyes, a rattling groan making his powerful body shake. "You should have told me that you're pregnant. You had so many opportunities, so many nights, so many—"

"I was scared that when you found out about this pregnancy, you would want me only for the baby. Never for me. I wanted you to want me for just myself, Apollo. And I'm sorry that I made you doubt me, that I…" Jia closed her eyes, wondering if she'd left it too late. If she'd burned down the little trust between them completely.

When she opened her eyes, he was gone. And that felt like a body blow to her.

After what felt like an eternity of waiting for him to return, she went back to the bed, grabbed the pillow and buried her face in it. Only a faint whiff of his scent was left in the fabric.

Fear clogged her throat, but she forced herself to breathe past it. She spent a few minutes talking to the bean in her belly, that their papa was angry but that she'd sort it out. All she had to do was wait out his very justified anger and tell him how much she loved him. At least she knew her own heart now.

She wanted a life with him, this wonderful, aching, real life with him. And she hoped he'd give her a chance to prove it to him. Because she knew now, beyond doubt, that he was happier than he'd ever been before, with her, that her pain had hurt him too, and that he loved her, even if he wouldn't admit it for the rest of their lives.

She had to have faith enough for the both of them.

CHAPTER TWELVE

AFTER A WHOLE week of Apollo not returning to the family home, or returning her calls, Jia decided she'd had enough. Yes, she'd hurt him, but couldn't he give her once chance to explain it? See it from her point of view? Understand that it had been her desperation to matter to him that had led her to hiding the truth?

Only now, when she was more rational, did she understand how deeply she'd hurt him. He expected her to abandon him like his father had done. And that was what she'd have done if knowing him and loving him hadn't changed her on a cellular level.

And maybe the only way to prove to him how much he meant to her was to leave this life and come back by her own choice.

And no matter what the state of her relationship, she wanted to attend her sister's wedding. She wanted a chance to build a new kind of relationship with her sister, who was doing her best to make amends.

So one bright chilly morning, Jia booked a flight, packed her bag and came downstairs to find Apollo's mother in the kitchen.

If she hadn't already cried enough to last a lifetime, she'd have fallen apart in front of this kind woman who even then had looked at her with nothing but understanding. Maria had wrapped her arms around Jia, kissed her temple, and gave her advice about how to combat the nausea and to take care of herself on the long flight.

She ran her hand over the dark wood of the banister, a bright glow of conviction in her heart.

This was her home, her family and her life with the man she adored with every breath. She wasn't abandoning it just when she'd realized how precious it was.

A day after Rina's wedding, Jia returned to their family home to collect a few things from her bedroom. Except for some books, keepsakes, and one large photo of her with her mom and Rina that she'd blown up and framed, she added the rest to a trash pile.

It was both fortifying and sad that she didn't need or want anything more from this home she'd lived in all her life. Everything that mattered, everything that she needed, Apollo had already given to her, a hundred times over.

She taped up the small cardboard box and brought it down to find her father, Vik and Rina waiting. For her.

For just a second, Jia wished for Apollo's presence so much that it was a physical ache in her belly. But no matter, she reminded herself, because he was there in her heart.

Rina strode to her side, hugged Jia and announced in that timid whisper of hers that she had a new job as a receptionist at a dental office. Jia had never been happier for her sister. Clearly, Michael was a great influence.

Vik, on the other hand, had a beard, dark shadows under his eyes and looked like he'd had a rough last few months. "I shouldn't have a laid a finger on either of you. Drunk or not," he said stiffly.

Jia nodded.

Her father, hands tucked into his coat pocket, looked as smart and stylish as he always did. But there was a beaten-down look in his eyes that made Jia wonder what new plague Apollo had unleashed on him. For so long, she'd done everything in her life to please this man. She'd yearned for one word of affection, for one hug, for one kind glance even.

"Is he treating you well, Jia?" he asked her, as if reading from a script he'd been asked to learn by rote. And suddenly, she wondered if this stilted, awkward reunion was all Apollo's doing.

Jia laughed, through the tears pooling in her eyes. "He's…good to me."

"About your stock," her father began.

"I don't want it," she said, shrugging. "I'll sell it to you for a dollar. Just tell me where to sign."

"I was about to tell you that it doesn't matter what you do with it. *He* already has controlling stock. He's had it for weeks now."

"What? How?"

Rina bit her lip, carefully avoiding their brother's and father's gazes. "I sold mine to him. Paul and I had nowhere to go and Dad had fired him. So I called Apollo and asked him if he wanted to buy it."

"My own daughter, selling out behind my back," Father said, with a flatness to his tone. It almost felt like…acceptance. Even regret maybe. "Not that I have ever done anything to earn any loyalty from either of you."

"What?" Jia asked, her mind reeling. "And he agreed?"

"Yes," Rina said, smiling. "He paid way over the market price. When I tried to protest, given he's your husband and I might need his help again, y'know," Rina said, winking in a very un-Rina way, "he said he needed this to be over. And then he turned around, appointed Dad the CEO again with some conditions, got Vik out of jail and—"

"When?"

"In the last couple of weeks. But he's not the controlling stock owner. You are," her father said, something almost like a smile twitching at his lips.

Jia had to reach for the pillar to steady herself. "What?"

"He said the only reason he wasn't also sending me to prison, for stealing from his father, for treating you with such…neglect was you. And the condition that he imposed was that I—"

"You treat me like a daughter you care about. As if I'm not the walking, talking symbol of your wife's infidelity," Jia said, giving voice to the words she'd wanted to for so long.

His father blanched. "I was wrong, Jia. On so many levels. And I'm here willingly to make any amends I can. I planned to fly out and see you even before Apollo began another level of upheaval in the company." Her father stared at his hands, and his mouth pursed. "I didn't realize what I had in you until I had nothing else."

Jia wanted to believe him. While he had never loved her as he should, he had never lied to her, or said a cross word to her either. And she did see the glimmer of truth in his eyes now. But, suddenly, his affection, his amends didn't matter much. Maybe she was just as good as Apollo at keeping grudges but right now, she had no bandwidth left to heal this particular relationship.

She simply nodded in his direction, bid her brother goodbye and left her childhood home with her happy sister by her side and a box full of memories.

Her heart was so full to bursting that she thought it might explode out of her chest. He had written the company he'd worked so hard to own into her name, he'd looked after them despite everything, had even forgiven the man he'd hated for years.

If there was a teeny pinch of doubt about his love for her, Jia had none now.

Jia had meant to fly out the same evening but when she'd gone back to the luxury hotel room she'd booked herself into, on Apollo's card, she found that she was exhausted. Every inch of her wanted to go back to him, to their bed, to their room, to that beautiful house where she'd discovered how much she loved him.

But after she'd showered, changed into one of Apollo's T-shirts that she'd carefully packed in her bag, and crawled into the large, luxurious king bed, sleep never came.

She turned and tossed for a couple of hours, then, finally sat up and ordered room service. Lunch had been a salad with Rina at one of their favorite places and she'd passed up dinner in pursuit of sleep.

When a knock came mere minutes later, she grabbed a robe, tied it and opened the door. To find Apollo standing there, his coat jacket on his arm.

Shirt buttons undone, a thick stubble on his jaw and his eyes wary with dark shadows cradling them, he looked rough and twisted inside out and some-how…incomplete. Exactly like she did.

Shaking from deep within, she opened the door wider and simply stood aside. Sudden, intense energy swathed what had felt like a vast space.

Jia watched as he threw the jacket on one of the chairs, paced the sitting lounge and then, after what felt like an eternity of seconds, came to face her. She, not having budged an inch from when she'd opened the door, pressed herself against it. She didn't feel fear, obviously. But something else. Something primal and so real that she felt dizzy under the weight of it.

"If you're angry that I came to New York anyway, let me explain," she started.

He shook his head. "I knew you would two minutes after I left our bedroom. And I've never, not even in that first moment, ever wanted to change who you are, or how you love so wholeheartedly. You're like a blazing sunset, *matia mou*. It was never... I wasn't trying to tell you that you couldn't see your bloody family. If you want, I'll arrange for them to—"

"I know that, Apollo. I also know that I broke the little tenuous trust you placed in me."

"Little and tenuous, *ágapi*? The sky itself couldn't contain the trust I have in you. The love I feel for you."

Jia trembled, and fought the sob rising up from her stomach, through her teeth like some great storm. But he stole that away too, filling her with shock when he went to his knees in front of her. "I'm sorry. I never ever meant to hurt you. I... I wanted you to love me. I wanted you to choose me for nothing but me. And I lost myself in that."

He leaned forward and pressed his mouth to her belly. "The thought of losing you and this baby and this..." a serrated growl left his mouth, his massive shoulders trembling like an evergreen bending under a gale "...turned me into that powerless, helpless monster again."

"Only I get to call you that. And after everything you did for my family...thank you."

"Thank you, Jia. It wasn't only for you, *ne*? It was

for us." Then he looked up and Jia cradled his cheeks and she thought she might faint at the love shining in his eyes. "You have released me from a prison of my own making. And suddenly, all I have is this over-powering, all-consuming need to adore you and love you and kiss you for the rest of our lives. Will you let me, Jia? Will you marry me again because I cannot imagine my life without you?"

Jia nodded and fell to her knees. He caught her and kissed her, and that sob she'd tried to hold off so hard broke through anyway.

Which of course made her grumpy husband very angry. He shot to his feet with her in his arms, brought her to the luxurious bed and held her in his lap, and clasped her jaw with a firm grip she loved. "No more tears, *agapi. Parakalo.* I can't bear to see them. I adore you, *yineka mou*, and if you continue to neglect your health, you will force me to—"

"I won't," Jia said, hiding her face in his throat.

"And will you take better care of yourself? Will you eat?"

"I want to eat," Jia said, giggling into his skin. "It's your little bean that uses my stomach as its very own washer and dryer."

Apollo looked up, stars and tears in his eyes, his palm covering her belly with a gentle reverence. "You're happy about this, then?"

Such anguish flickered through the question that Jia had to swallow before she spoke. "Yes. Absolutely. I want this, with you. I want to have at least two more and I want us to love them as much as we love each other, and play with them, and hug them and teach them how to build castles. But more than anything, more than even this, Apollo, I want a life with you. I want to love you and be loved by you. Forever and ever."

"All of it, and so much more, it's all yours, Jia. I'm all yours."

She buried her face in his chest and clung to him while he pressed tender, reverent kisses up and down her temple, jaw and neck.

Finally, after what felt like hours but was mere minutes, her heart settled. Especially when he pulled her under him and began to lavish her with kisses and promises.

EPILOGUE

THREE WEEKS LATER, as afternoon gave way to early evening, Jia tried her best not to steal a glance out the bedroom's window at Apollo's, no, their family home.

While she'd spent most of the afternoon napping and daydreaming and drooling over Apollo's sweatshirt that she'd wrapped around herself—because he'd been gone for the last three days arranging her surprise—Christina came in to help her get ready.

Which wasn't really necessary. Yes, Jia was showing, because the bean was growing at a steady, good pace, but Apollo's sisters and mom and he himself, of course, treated her like she was the first one in the entire galaxy to give birth.

Anticipation fluttering through her, she pulled on loose jeans and a lacy, flowy top that flared from under her breasts to still give her a nice shape. The top was a shimmery ivory silk with pearl beading along its neckline, a gift from Chiara. Jia had laughed when she'd opened the package, because Apollo's sister finally seemed to have understood that she was never going to get Jia to wear frilly, over-the-top dresses.

In the week since he'd told her, Jia hadn't asked Apollo what the surprise was and it had come at extreme risk, since no one in her life had ever taunted her with one. But, knowing that getting this right was really important for her everything-must-be-perfect husband in this new, fragile, overwhelming stage of their relationship, she had stopped trying to coerce various family members into spilling the secret.

When she came down the stairs, her eyes widened. The entire house had been lit up with soft fairy lights and was overflowing with extended family and friends—most she was beginning to recognize now. Uniformed waiters weaved around the crowd with serving trays filled with champagne and other drinks. For a split second, Jia thought she'd seen her father and sister but she was being pulled along.

Congratulations and cheers surrounded her, with that great-aunt and this uncle interrupting them on their way to the backyard. Standing at the entrance to the patio, Jia spied the large white marquee. And past the white marquee, following the cleared walking trail, an arch had been set up with lilies and white roses curving around it, along with twinkling lights. Behind it was the gentle lapping of the ocean and above her, a canopy of stars, as if the sky itself had decided to put on a show.

No, as if it had been commanded to put on a show by her grumpy beast of a husband.

Breath hitching, Jia walked down the steps, only to find that a path had been made up of red rose petals toward the arch. As if someone had orchestrated it by magic, every single guest settled into their chair.

"Jia?"

She turned to find her father, trying his best to not crowd her.

"May I give you away, please?"

While their relationship would never be the one she'd imagined, the new one—mostly repaired and forged by his efforts—was not bad. Tears filling her eyes, she nodded. And on the way, she spied her sister, her eyes bright and shining.

And there, at the end of the small path, standing in a black Armani suit that made him so gorgeous that her knees buckled, was Apollo. Jia forgot everything, everyone as she stared up at him.

She could feel his eyes travel down her length and he laughed as they lingered on her top and jeans. When his gaze swept back up, pausing just for a second on her chest, to her hair, pleasure suffused her. "Will you not come to me, Jia?" he said, extending his arm out to her. But even the darkness couldn't mask the hoarse tremble in his voice.

"You should have told me what you were planning," she whispered, beyond overjoyed.

"And have you show up in some frilly dress that's not you? I adore you as you are, *pethi mou*. And I wanted to give you a wedding under the stars."

Jia breathed hard, awed again by this man who heard every sleepy wish and dream she mumbled about. So, she went to him, her heart already given over to him.

"You take my breath away, *yineka mou*," he said, lifting her knuckles to his mouth and pressing a soft kiss. "And nothing, nothing, in the world has ever rendered me so."

And now she could see his face that she adored so much—that high forehead, and the arrogant thrust of his nose and those wide, thin lips that had kissed and caressed every inch of her in desire and affection and…reverence.

Then she turned to look out over the grounds and he was behind her, his arms coming around to rest on her belly again. He was going to do that a lot, Jia realized. Their guests laughed at their unconventional behavior but then they didn't know that she was the one who had proposed this marriage to the man she adored.

"You're ready to marry me again, then?" Apollo murmured in her ear.

"Yes, please. Now," she whispered and then with her hand in his, she followed him toward a life that she knew would never be lonely or empty or unloved. Even past the contract deadline.

* * * * *

Did you fall in love with Contractually Wed?
*Then why not try these other fabulous stories
by Tara Pammi?*

The Reason for His Wife's Return
An Innocent's Deal with the Devil
Saying "I Do" to the Wrong Greek
Twins to Tame Him
Fiancée for the Cameras

Available now!